# IS LISA LEAVING HOME?

"Wentworth Manor is one of the most famous girls' schools in the country, dear. We're very lucky to have gotten an interview for you," Mrs. Atwood said.

"Where is it?" Lisa asked.

"It's in Richfield, about two hours from Willow Creek."

"But I don't get it, " Lisa said, taken aback. "Are we moving?"

Mrs. Atwood laughed. "Oh, no, dear. Your father and I are very happy in Willow Creek."

"Then why am I having an interview at a school if there's no chance I would ever go to it?" Lisa asked. Her mother had had some wild ideas in the past, but this one was the wildest yet.

"It's a boarding school," Mrs. Atwood explained patiently. "The girls live at the school."

Lisa stared at her mother in alarm. "When did you decide you wanted me to go to boarding school?" she asked, shocked.

"It's only an interview, honey. If you don't like it—"

"But Mom," Lisa interrupted, "why would you want me to leave home?"

THE SADDLE CLUB

# WILD HORSES

## BONNIE BRYANT

A SKYLARK BOOK
NEW YORK · TORONTO · LONDON · SYDNEY · AUCKLAND

RL 5, 009–012

WILD HORSES

A Bantam Skylark Book / September 1996

ISBN 0-553-48371-4

Published simultaneously in the United States and Canada.

PRINTED IN THE UNITED STATES OF AMERICA

OPM      0 9 8 7 6 5 4 3 2 1

*I would like to express my special thanks
to Caitlin Macy for her help
in the writing of this book.*

"But, Stevie, there just has to be *something* good about going back to school!" Lisa Atwood cried. When it came to school, Lisa and Stevie Lake were opposites. Stevie utterly detested it and always got into trouble. Lisa enjoyed it and brought home straight As.

"Nope." Stevie shook her head defiantly. "There's not. I've thought and thought, and there's not one single reason why I, Stephanie Lake, should be glad that the summer's over."

The two girls were sitting on hay bales at Pine Hollow Stables with their other best friend, Carole Hanson. Pine Hollow was the stable where they all took riding lessons and where Stevie and Carole boarded their horses. Carole was in the middle about school. She didn't hate it or love it; she got through and did fine. Once in a while she even became interested enough in something she was learning to forget about horses—for about five seconds.

"Maybe you just need time to readjust—you know, have a few days to let it sink in, the way Lisa and I have," Carole suggested. She tried not to sound as doubtful as she felt. Carole and Lisa went to the local public junior high school. They had been back a week already, but Stevie went to Fenton Hall, a private school, which had started only the day before.

"Yeah, right. I'll be too excited for words in another week or two," Stevie muttered sarcastically.

"Aren't there any teachers you like?" Lisa asked. "Or at least any teachers you don't detest?" she corrected herself. To ask if Stevie *liked* a teacher was like asking someone if she *liked* having to eat spinach and liver every day for nine months out of the year.

Stevie sighed, plucking wisps of hay out of the bale. "It's easy for you to look on the bright side, Lisa. You enjoy school. You probably even *love* school. I would, too, if I were you. You ace every subject. You're a teacher's dream."

2

Lisa laughed at Stevie's hopeless expression. She wasn't so sure she *loved* school, but it was easy to at least like something she was so good at. She was friendly with her teachers and looked forward to the school day. And since she was a real perfectionist, she also liked seeing her report card come in with all As.

"I'm not even happy to see the other kids," Stevie went on grumpily. "I'm sick of them. I've known all of them my whole life. Plus the fact that everywhere I went today, I saw you-know-who."

Carole and Lisa nodded, smiling knowingly. Stevie could only be referring to one person, and that was Pine Hollow's biggest snob, Veronica diAngelo. All the girls knew Veronica from riding with her, but Stevie had to put up with seeing her at Fenton Hall, too. Veronica was vain and stuck-up. She was also rude—rude to everyone and especially rude to The Saddle Club, the group that Stevie, Lisa, and Carole had started. Fortunately, Veronica could never be a member of The Saddle Club.

There were two requirements for joining the club, and Veronica failed on both accounts: She wasn't horse-crazy, and she certainly wasn't willing to help people out when they needed it. Sure, she rode a lot, but as The Saddle Club knew, riding by itself didn't qualify a person as horse-crazy. To be horse-crazy, a person had to love everything about horses: riding, training, grooming, stable work—everything. The main reason Veronica rode was that it was a glamorous sport. It was something she could brag about to her friends and her parents could brag about to their friends.

"So, there aren't even any cute boys at school?" Carole asked. Even though Stevie had a boyfriend, Carole knew she wasn't above enjoying having cute boys in her classes.

"The only thing I can say about the boys is that they make Chad, Michael, and Alex look like princes," Stevie said, referring to her three brothers, whom she was constantly feuding with. Then Stevie perked up. "But if there *were* any cute boys, I guess there would be one good thing about being back at school. I just remembered: There's going to be a back-to-school dance in a couple of weeks. They announced it in Assembly this morning."

"I told you so," Lisa said. "Now that sounds really fun."

"It will be," Stevie predicted. "As long as the dance committee does its job and makes it fun. I wish you guys and Phil could come. Why do dances have to be school only?" Phil Marsten was Stevie's boyfriend. He rode, too, and lived in a neighboring town. "We could have so much fun. The three of us could all get ready together on the night of the dance. Do our hair, choose our out-fits—"

"Oh my gosh!" Lisa exclaimed, springing up. "I forgot! I have a hair appointment this afternoon. I was supposed to call my mother the minute we were done riding so she could pick me up!"

Just then there was a loud honk in the driveway. A woman's voice called, "Lisa! Honey?"

"Sounds like your mom knew where to find you," Carole said with a laugh, recognizing Mrs. Atwood's voice.

"Phew! So, I'll see you guys tomorrow?" Lisa said.

"Same time, same place," Stevie said. It was practically an unwritten rule that The Saddle Club always hung out at Pine Hollow after school.

"Where are you getting your hair cut?" Carole asked as Lisa gathered up her things.

Lisa paused. "Umm . . . Cosmopolitan Cuts," she mumbled.

"Cosmo Cuts?" Stevie repeated. "Isn't that the new salon on Pelham Street that the famous stylist owns?" she demanded.

Lisa nodded sheepishly.

"Wow! My mom went there last month. She said it was supernice and superexpensive," said Stevie. "They give you the royal treatment there. I think you get a free makeover the first time you go."

"I just remembered why I've heard of it. Veronica goes there, doesn't she?" Carole said. "I think I heard her bragging about it."

Stevie nodded. "Yup. And she *only* goes to Charles, the owner. She won't have her hair cut by any of his assistants. Are you going to have Charles, Lisa?"

"I don't know," Lisa said shortly. "My mother made the appointment."

"Wow, pretty fancy-schmancy, Lisa," Stevie teased.

All at once Carole noticed how uncomfortable Lisa looked. She shot Stevie a meaningful look. "Have fun, okay, Lisa?" she said.

"I will," Lisa promised, heading down the aisle to the door.

"Why the look? Did I say something wrong?" Stevie asked when Lisa was safely out of earshot.

"No, not really," Carole replied. "But we both know what Mrs. Atwood is like. I think Lisa gets embarrassed sometimes about all the things her mother makes her do."

Stevie nodded. She knew exactly what Carole meant. Even though the Atwoods didn't have a lot of money, Mrs. Atwood was very socially conscious. She always tried to make Lisa do the "right" things. In the past she'd made Lisa take all kinds of lessons, such as tennis and ballet. She also liked her daughter to wear coordinated outfits like a model in a catalog. And no matter how many times Lisa tried to tell her mother how awful Veronica diAngelo was, Mrs. Atwood didn't seem to hear. She admired the diAngelos for being so rich and well connected in Willow Creek, the town where they lived in Virginia.

It was just like Mrs. Atwood to take Lisa to the expensive new hair salon. If Stevie had told *her* mother that she wanted to go to Cosmo Cuts, Mrs. Lake would have burst out laughing.

"Speaking of haircuts," Carole said, "let's go finish pulling Delilah's mane."

"Good idea. We'd better do it before Max gets finished with his lesson or he'll think we've been sitting on these hay bales all afternoon talking," Stevie replied. The Saddle Club was so used to helping out at Pine Hollow that the stable's owner, Max Regnery, not only expected it but demanded it. Before their afternoon ride, the girls had started to use a metal comb to pull out the long hairs from one of the horses' manes. Now the mane was half short and half long.

"If we don't get it done soon, Delilah will be the one who needs that free makeover," Carole kidded as she and Stevie went to get the mare.

*  *  *

LISA LEANED BACK in the front seat of the car and watched the pleasant suburban scenery roll by. Her mother was chatting excitedly about all the prominent women in Willow Creek who had started going to Cosmo Cuts. Lisa didn't care, so she pretended to listen while losing herself in her own thoughts. She was glad her mother had come to pick her up even though Lisa had forgotten to call. Lisa hated to disappoint her mother. Even a small thing like forgetting to call could make her mother feel bad. She tried so hard to give Lisa the best of everything, even though they didn't have a lot of money, that Lisa hated to let her down.

The haircut was a perfect example. Her mother had been all excited about taking Lisa there. Lisa had always been perfectly happy going to the walk-in place at the Willow Creek mall, but when she saw how much it meant to her mother to switch to Cosmo Cuts, she had let her make the appointment. It wasn't that big a deal—it was just typical of the way things went between them.

Cosmo Cuts was as elegant as Stevie had predicted. To Lisa it looked more like someone's living room than a hair salon. After Mrs. Atwood disappeared with the makeup consultant, Lisa sat on a plush couch in the entry area waiting for her appointment. She looked around curiously. The main room was bustling with chic, well-dressed women, many in business suits. Some were getting their hair cut, some were sitting under dryers, some were having manicures.

It was easy to tell who the famous Charles was. All the women chatted with him, no matter who was cutting their hair. He kept up a running conversation with half a dozen people, meanwhile styling his own client's hair. The only other girl Lisa's age was whining loudly to her mother as her hair was shampooed. Lisa listened in when she overheard the topic of conversation.

"Why can't I have my own horse, Mother? Daddy said I could!" the girl wailed.

"Because you have to take riding lessons first," the mother replied curtly.

"If you're interested in riding lessons," another woman spoke up from across the room, "the only place to go is Pine Hollow."

"Watch it, Claire, keep your head steady," Charles reprimanded the elegant, gray-haired woman.

"I completely agree," said a third woman who was having her hair dyed blond. "The diAngelo girl rides there, you know."

"Is that true?" said the girl's mother. "She rides at Pine Hollow?"

"Absolutely. I hear she's the star pupil. And Pine Hollow might not look as fancy as Clover Farm or Hilldale, but that Max Regnery runs a tight ship, I'll tell you."

"You said it," said the other woman. "And he's not bad-looking, either."

"Didn't he marry that journalist from out of town?" Charles asked.

"Oh yes. They had a small, private ceremony at the farm. I hear—"

Lisa couldn't stop herself from giggling. She wondered what Max would say if he knew he was being gossiped about at Cosmo Cuts. And it was too funny that the women thought Veronica was the star pupil! That was one rumor that had obviously been started by either Veronica or her mother. Before Lisa could muse any longer, a woman brought her a smock to put on over her clothes. "We're ready for you now, Ms. Atwood," she said.

For the next hour, Lisa thought of nothing but how much fun it was to go to a luxurious salon like Cosmo Cuts. She had a shampoo, a conditioning treatment, a cut by one of Charles's assistants, a blow-dry, and, since she didn't wear makeup, a complimentary manicure instead.

"So, what do you think?" Lisa's mother asked her when they were heading out to the car. "Wasn't it wonderful?"

Lisa weighed her words carefully. The afternoon *had* been a wonderful treat. Her haircut, however, came out the same way it always did, but for thirty dollars more. Lisa didn't want to be ungrateful or say anything that would burst her mother's bubble. "It was—really nice. Thanks a lot, Mom," she said finally.

"I'm so glad you liked it!" Mrs. Atwood exclaimed. "I wanted you to look nice for your interview Saturday."

Lisa looked sharply at her mother. "What interview?" she asked suspiciously. Mrs. Atwood had been known to sign Lisa up for things without telling her. This was the first Lisa had heard of any interview.

"Didn't I tell you?" Mrs. Atwood asked. "We're going to Wentworth Manor this weekend. We're going to take a tour and then you're going to have an interview."

Lisa frowned. She wasn't sure she understood. She thought she'd heard of Wentworth before, but she couldn't say where. "What, exactly, is Wentworth Manor, and why am I having an interview there?" she asked.

"Wentworth Manor is one of the most famous girls' schools in the country, dear. We're very lucky to have gotten an interview for you," Mrs. Atwood replied.

"Where is it?" Lisa asked.

"It's in Richfield, about two hours from Willow Creek."

11

"But I don't get it," Lisa said, taken aback. "Are we moving?"

Mrs. Atwood laughed. "Oh, no, dear. Your father and I are very happy in Willow Creek."

"Then why am I having an interview at a school if there's no chance I would ever go to it?" Lisa asked. Her mother had had some wild ideas in the past, but this one was the wildest yet.

"It's a boarding school," Mrs. Atwood explained patiently. "The girls live at the school."

Lisa stared at her mother in alarm. "When did you decide you wanted me to go to boarding school?" she asked, shocked.

"It's only an interview, honey. If you don't like it—"

"But Mom," Lisa interrupted, "why would you want me to leave home?"

"We don't *want* you to leave home, but we would *let* you for your own benefit. And even having the interview is a wonderful opportunity that you should be grateful for." Mrs. Atwood's voice sounded a bit severe.

Lisa tried to formulate a response, but she couldn't think fast enough. She was completely floored by her mother's announcement.

Mrs. Atwood pursed her lips. "Look, probably nothing will come of this, but the school is interested in seeing you, and I arranged for you to have an interview, all

12

right? Wentworth is right in the heart of Virginia horse country, you know. Who knows? You may love it." With that, she unlocked the car doors and climbed into the driver's seat.

Lisa got in on her side. She was silent as her mother started the car and pulled out into the street. Her head was reeling. This had to be the most far-fetched idea her mother had ever had. Lisa could no sooner imagine herself going to a boarding school than she could imagine going to the moon! But then she realized something: Boarding schools cost thousands and thousands of dollars. A nice haircut now and then was one thing, but prep-school tuition was quite another.

"Uh, Mom?" she began cautiously. "Don't schools like Wentworth cost a lot?"

Mrs. Atwood looked exasperated. "Well, ye-es. Anyway, the point is, we'll have to see how you like it first," she said briskly. "I thought you could spend some time with the girls to get a feel for the place. Maybe Saturday afternoon they could take you to see the stables. Imagine that, Lisa, the famous Wentworth stables! I know you've heard of them. I hear they're magnificent." She reached over and gave Lisa's hand an excited squeeze.

Lisa stared at her mother again, but her mother's eyes were fixed on the road. She had her I-won't-take-no-for-an-answer look on her face. Lisa knew she ought to put

13

an end to the whole idea right away. It would only upset her mother when she realized that they could never afford to send Lisa to the school and that even if they could, she would never want to go. Then Lisa had a second thought. Why should she ruin her mother's plans after she had gone to so much trouble? One day at Wentworth wasn't going to kill her. And now that she knew that it was the same Wentworth whose stables she had heard so much about, it might be interesting to see.

Besides, when it came right down to it, Lisa knew, she had absolutely nothing to worry about. For the first time in her life, she was glad beyond belief that her parents weren't rich. With a resigned sigh, she sat back in her seat. "It sounds like fun, Mom," she said.

STEVIE GROANED IN self-pity. Here it was, only the third day of the term, and she couldn't wait for summer vacation. Even though it was Friday, it had been the worst possible day imaginable. She'd missed the bus because she hadn't been able to find her science book. Her mother had been annoyed that she had to drive Stevie to school and had lectured her the entire way. Then she'd been late anyway. Everybody had made jokes about Stevie's being tardy on only the third day. Then her science teacher had made a joke about her forgetting her book on only the third day. "But I didn't forget it, Ms.

Anderson, I *lost* it!" Stevie had said, before she realized how much worse that sounded.

In sports they had to do the fifty-yard dash. To the delight of Veronica diAngelo, Stevie had tripped and fallen and had the slowest time in the class, when usually she was in the top ten. At lunch, seeing signs in the cafeteria for the back-to-school dance had cheered her up the tiniest bit—until Alex and Chad informed her that the boys had decided the Fenton dances were lame and were planning to boycott this one.

For the final straw, now that the school day was over and she was about to escape to Pine Hollow, where she could share her miseries with Lisa and Carole, Stevie had found a note taped to her locker. Not just any note, but a note from the headmistress of the school: *Stevie, Please see me before you leave for the day—Miss Fenton.*

Walking down the hall to the headmistress's office, Stevie racked her brains, trying to figure out why she was in trouble. The only thing she could remember doing was telling Veronica that her new outfit made her look like walking wallpaper. Could Miss Fenton have found out about that? It would be just like Veronica to tell on Stevie. Maybe Stevie could feign innocence, or better yet, pretend she'd meant it as a compliment. Waiting on the bench outside the office, Stevie composed an extravagant explanation. After a few minutes, Miss Fenton opened her door. She summoned Stevie inside.

"Now, Stephanie—"

"I know, Miss Fenton," Stevie said breathlessly. "I know how bad it *sounds*, but, you see, I meant it as a compliment! I love wallpaper! Why, you should see the wallpaper at our house. It's beautiful—all bright and flowery. How was I supposed to know she would take it the wrong way? I mean, I *am* sorry, but I really don't think—"

"Stephanie, what in heaven's name are you talking about?" Miss Fenton broke in.

Stevie smiled wanly. "You mean this isn't about the wallpaper?"

"What wallpaper?" Miss Fenton demanded.

"Never mind—no wallpaper. You can forget all about the wallpaper, Miss Fenton," Stevie croaked.

Miss Fenton sat down at her desk. She motioned for Stevie to sit down, too. She folded her hands, raised her right eyebrow, and looked sternly at Stevie. "If you mean to tell me that you and Veronica diAngelo are feuding already, I don't want to hear about it. Put an end to it at once."

"But—"

"Keep your distance from one another if you must."

17

"Yes, Miss Fenton," Stevie said, trying to sound contrite. "May I go now?"

"Go? No, you may not. I called you in here for a purpose, not for my own amusement. Would you like to hear why?"

"Yes, Miss Fenton," said Stevie. She crossed her fingers, hoping the headmistress's "purpose" wouldn't be a huge pain.

"All right, then. I'm making you head of the back-to-school dance committee."

Stevie sat forward in her chair. "Really? But what about the old dance committee?" For as long as Stevie had been going to the Fenton dances, the same handful of older boys and girls had been running them.

"They don't want to do it anymore. With the boys threatening to boycott, they don't feel appreciated. Besides, it's time for some new blood. So I'm placing you at the helm. You'll have to choose a cochair. The two of you will then pick a theme and organize the decorations, music, and refreshments. Naturally you can recruit other volunteers, too. Make sure you include some boys. And there's not much time. Got it?"

"Got it," Stevie said, flabbergasted. "But why me?"

Miss Fenton smiled for the first time. "It has come to my attention that you have a knack for organizing,

Stephanie. I'm trusting you to put some life into this back-to-school dance."

"Don't worry, Miss Fenton. I won't let you down," Stevie said promptly. "The kids will go wild, I promise."

"Not too wild, I hope. You also have to find parents to chaperone," Miss Fenton reminded her. "So, off you go. Keep me posted, all right?"

With that, Miss Fenton showed Stevie the door. Stevie was so excited, she skipped down the almost deserted hallway. She had never felt so appreciated at school before. Being head of the dance committee was a big honor. The students who had done it before were always looked up to by the younger kids. They had a real presence in the school. They also had privileges like getting to skip gym to work on decorations. But the main reason Stevie was so excited by the news was that she knew she would be great at the job. This must be the way Lisa felt before she took a test, Stevie figured. "I'm sure going to ace this one!" she said aloud.

"What did you say, Stevie?" a girl asked, emerging from a classroom.

Stevie stopped and turned. She recognized a girl from Veronica's crowd. "Hi, Sarah. I was just saying how happy I am that Miss Fenton asked me to be head of the dance committee," she said nonchalantly.

19

"You are?" the girl said. "But what about last year's committee?"

"They quit," Stevie replied cheerfully.

"They did? Wow. But wait, aren't there usually two heads?" the girl asked.

Stevie nodded. "Yes. I still have to pick someone to help me. Tough decision, huh?"

The girl looked serious. "Very. But, you know, I think I heard Veronica saying today that she was interested in the job. It's funny that Miss Fenton didn't pick her, but now you can. She'd be a great cochair."

Stevie almost laughed out loud, but she managed to keep a straight face. "Thanks, Sarah. I'll keep her in mind, okay?" Once the girl had gone, Stevie had to giggle. Veronica would make the worst cochair imaginable! She would want to do it only for the recognition. She hated to work hard at anything. Her idea of adding some life to something was to spend a lot of money buying stuff. But she always surrounded herself with shallow people like Sarah, who worshipped her. "That'll be the day," Stevie muttered to herself. "Sure, I'll make Veronica cochair—when horses get wings!"

"WHAT ON EARTH do you think could have happened to Stevie?" Carole asked. She and Lisa were schooling their horses, Starlight and Prancer, in the outdoor ring.

Lisa didn't actually own Prancer, but she had ridden the mare for a long time, so it was almost as if she did. As a favor to Stevie, who was late, the girls had groomed her horse, Belle, and left her tacked up in her stall, expecting that Stevie would show up right away. But almost an hour had passed, and she hadn't arrived. Carole and Lisa had warmed up. Now they were starting to work on a few dressage movements.

"You don't think she could have detention already, do you?" Lisa asked.

"It wouldn't exactly shock me," Carole said, grinning as she sat down in the saddle to ask Starlight for a canter. She kept the young bay half-Thoroughbred in a small circle at first, asking him to bend around the turns. After a couple of circles, she cantered down the diagonal of the ring. In the middle she asked for a flying change. Starlight responded by switching leads in midair.

"Wow, Carole, he looks great," Lisa called. She followed Carole's example, but instead of doing a flying change, she had Prancer break to a trot in the middle of the ring and then pick up the new lead. Even though Prancer had come a long way from her days as a fresh-off-the-track ex-racehorse, Lisa tried to keep things simple when she could, to help build the mare's confidence. She knew there was no point in rushing a horse's training; it would only backfire later.

21

"Nice job," Carole said, returning Lisa's compliment. The two girls trotted together down the long side of the ring. "I guess in a way it's back to school for the horses, too," said Lisa. "The summer is always so crazy with Pony Club and camp and shows that it seems like there's no time for quiet schooling until September."

"I know," Carole agreed, slowing Starlight to a walk. "I don't want to jump for a week or so. I want to concentrate on dressage. Maybe we can all stay late after Horse Wise tomorrow and work on a few things together," she suggested. Horse Wise was the local branch of the United States Pony Club. All The Saddle Club girls were members.

Lisa frowned in annoyance. "I'm not going to be here. Maybe somebody else could ride Prancer so she gets exercised."

"Where are you going?" asked Carole. It was unusual for Lisa to miss a day of riding, not to mention a Pony Club lesson.

Lisa looked embarrassed. "It's so stupid," she began. "I—I have to go to Wentworth Manor."

"Wentworth Manor? Why? Is there a clinic there or something?" Carole asked. Professional riders often taught special riding classes at big stables such as the one at Wentworth. "Should we all go?"

Lisa shook her head. "I wish it were a riding clinic.

Actually—you see—the truth is, my mother's making me interview there," she finished in a rush.

Carole looked at her. "You mean she wants you to go to school there?" she asked, surprised. Carole never even thought of Wentworth Manor as a school. She knew the stables were connected to a boarding school, but it had never actually occurred to her that girls from places like Willow Creek went there.

Lisa nodded unhappily. "It's so stupid, Carole. We could never afford it, and I would never want to go there, but my mother gets these ideas in her head . . ."

Carole listened sympathetically—she knew how pushy Mrs. Atwood could be. Sometimes she was outwardly pushy, and other times she was pushy in a different way—the "guilt-trip" kind of pushy. She could make Lisa feel bad if Lisa didn't do as she asked.

"Anyway, at least I only have to visit the place. And the drive there is supposed to be nice. It goes right by a bunch of the famous horse farms," Lisa concluded.

Carole had been about to suggest that Lisa tell her mother how she felt, but she decided not to. She didn't want to interfere, especially if Lisa had already worked everything out in her head. After all, Lisa was her mother's daughter, and if anyone knew how to handle Mrs. Atwood, it was probably Lisa. Carole changed the topic and asked Lisa about her haircut.

"It was great!" said Lisa.

"I guess it will be all crushed from your hat, but I'll have to see it after we ride," Carole said enthusiastically.

Lisa hastened to set her straight. "Actually, my hair doesn't look very different. It's just the salon itself that was so much fun." She filled Carole in on the luxurious setting and the funny gossip she'd overheard.

"Star pupil!" Carole said indignantly when Lisa got to the part about Veronica. "Star of her own universe, more like."

The two girls laughed and then split up again to work individually with their horses. When they headed to the barn half an hour later, Stevie still had not arrived. Lisa had to go to a ballet lesson, so Carole volunteered to untack Belle. "Great, and if you see Stevie, will you explain to her why I'm not coming tomorrow?" Lisa asked. "I left a note for Max explaining about Pony Club."

"Sure, and call us tomorrow night and tell us all about it, okay?" Carole said.

When Lisa had gone, Carole gave Starlight a final pat and went to Belle's stall. "Poor thing, we got you all tacked up for nothing," Carole said, unbuckling the mare's girth. Belle champed her bit impatiently. Usually tack meant going out for a ride; instead she'd been waiting in her stall for an hour.

"Stevie's not around?" a voice inquired.

Carole looked up to see Max's mother, Mrs. Reg, looking over the stall door. The older woman was a good friend of The Saddle Club and often stopped to chat with the girls on her stable rounds.

"She was supposed to ride with Lisa and me, but she never made it," Carole explained.

"If I know Stevie Lake, she's up to some scheming," Mrs. Reg said with a chuckle. She knew all the girls' personalities well—sometimes too well. She often knew what was going on with them before they knew it themselves.

"Say, Mrs. Reg," Carole said, laying Belle's saddle gently over the wall of the stall. "Have you ever heard of Wentworth Manor?"

"Wentworth? Of course," Mrs. Reg said. "They've got one of the nicest facilities in Virginia. Sixty horses, hundreds of acres . . ."

"No, I mean the school. What's it like?"

"Oh, the school. Right. We horsey people tend to forget it exists, don't we?" Mrs. Reg said.

"We sure do," Carole agreed. "I guess because the stables are so well known."

"Yes, but that's not the only reason. The stables are fantastic; the school itself isn't so hot."

"Really?" Carole said.

"Yes, you know—it's one of those snobby riding schools. Rich girls go there so they can keep riding and showing. At least, that was its reputation in my day. It may have changed—improved its academics—but I don't know. Why do you ask?"

"Oh, no particular reason," Carole said lightly. "Just curious."

Mrs. Reg gave her a penetrating look. "You're not thinking of going there, are you?"

"Oh no!" Carole exclaimed. "Of course not, Mrs. Reg."

"Good. Because you can get a much better education right here in Willow Creek," Mrs. Reg said firmly.

"And a much better riding education right here at Pine Hollow, right?" Carole kidded her.

"That, my dear, goes without saying," Mrs. Reg said with a wink.

"HOLD IT RIGHT there," a voice said.

Carole turned, body brush in hand, from grooming Belle. "Hey, I thought you weren't coming," she said, happy to see Stevie's pert face over the stall door.

"I thought I wasn't coming, too, but then I figured there was still time to have a quick ride in the indoor ring," Stevie said.

"Well, Belle's all groomed, so hand me that saddle and I'll put it back on," Carole said promptly.

Stevie picked the saddle up and gave it to Carole. The girls helped one another out on so many occasions that Stevie didn't need to thank Carole for grooming Belle, but she did anyway. Somehow when Carole brushed a horse, it took on an extra glow. Stevie was sure her friend doused her body brush with magic gleaming powder, but Carole insisted it was elbow grease, pure and simple. "Thanks to you, Carole, Belle looks just like her name—a beautiful Southern belle. Don't you, girl?" Stevie murmured, giving the half-Saddlebred a pat on her neck.

"All right, cut the cute stuff and tell me why you're so late," Carole said. "It better be good."

Stevie grinned. "Thought you'd never ask. But first we've got to find Lisa. I want her to hear, too."

"Lisa's gone for the day," Carole told her.

"Already? Oh, well, I guess I can catch her tomorrow."

"Nope. She won't be here then, either."

"Really? Why not?"

"Her mother is taking her to look at Wentworth Manor," Carole said. She watched Stevie's face to see how she would react.

Stevie looked perplexed. "What? Did I hear that right? Why would Lisa look at Wentworth?"

Carole shrugged. "I don't know, but her mother set up an interview for her."

"You're *kidding*!" Stevie exclaimed.

Belle threw her head up in annoyance at Stevie's

raised voice. Down the aisle came another voice: "No need to announce your presence to the whole stable, Stevie," Max barked.

Stevie grimaced slightly, but even a reprimand from Max couldn't distract her. "Can we talk about this for a minute?" she asked, looking around for somewhere private.

"Locker room?" Carole suggested. Stevie nodded. They left Belle tied in her stall with the saddle on and went to the locker room at the other end of the stable. The girls kept their riding clothes there and used the room to change in before lessons. They also used it for the occasional private conference.

Once inside, Stevie closed the door. "Am I getting this right?"

"Yes," Carole said. "Lisa's mother is making her have an interview at Wentworth Manor."

Stevie groaned. "Carole, do you realize that Wentworth Manor is the biggest snob school in the state? It's horrible! The girls are so rich they're scary."

"It's that bad?" Carole asked. Stevie's reaction confirmed what Mrs. Reg had said.

"Let me just say that my brothers call it Worth-a-lot Manor. Do you think Mrs. Atwood actually wants Lisa to go to *school* there?"

"It looks that way, but—"

29

"But what about Lisa? She doesn't want to go, does she? I mean, she couldn't."

Carole shook her head. "No, listen, Stevie. From what Lisa said, she's only going to the interview so her mother doesn't get upset. There's no chance of her ever actually going there. She said her parents could never afford a school like that." Carole paused, suddenly alarmed. "She's right about that . . . isn't she?"

Stevie sat down on a bench to think for a minute. "It *is* supposed to be one of the most expensive schools around," she said slowly. "Which isn't surprising, considering they have one of the nicest riding stables. I know it costs a heck of a lot more than being a day student at Fenton Hall, that's for sure."

"Do you know anyone who goes there?" Carole asked.

"Thankfully, no. I know *of* one girl—she used to go to Fenton, but her parents moved to Washington, D.C., after third grade. I think I heard she was going to Wentworth now. Wait, I remember: When she lived here, she was best friends with Veronica. Veronica was talking about her awhile ago—as if I'd care that her ex–best friend goes to Wentworth," Stevie said derisively. "So I don't really know anyone there. But Fenton sometimes plays Wentworth in sports tournaments. The girls are the worst. They're real crybabies if they don't win."

"It sounds terrible," Carole said. She couldn't even

30

imagine going to a school like Wentworth. Willow Creek Junior High had its ups and downs, and she certainly liked some of the kids better than others, but it was a normal school—not some snob factory!

"It is terrible. If I'd known, I would have tried to convince Lisa to not even waste her time this weekend," Stevie said.

"I think it's easier for her to just go. Otherwise, she'd have to have a big fight with her mother about it," Carole said.

"Which she would never do," Stevie said, finishing Carole's thought. Lisa didn't fight with her parents, especially her mother. She hated to upset them, so she usually just gave in. She thought it was easier that way. "So she'll be back Saturday night?" Stevie asked.

Carole nodded. "Yeah, I told her to call us the minute she gets in."

"Good, we can set her straight then, if she hasn't figured out how awful Wentworth is on her own."

"Stevie," Carole said gently, "don't cut it down too much. It will only make Lisa feel bad if she ends up liking it and can't go there."

"Don't worry—she won't like it," Stevie replied firmly. "Would you want to go to a school filled with . . ." Stevie stopped without finishing her sentence. She had been about to say "filled with Veroni-

31

cas," but right that second, the door opened and Veronica herself walked in.

"Talking about me as usual?" Veronica asked, her voice saccharine-sweet. "Really, can't you two think of another topic?"

Stevie returned Veronica's huge, fake smile with an even huger, faker one of her own. "We were just leaving, actually. It's too crowded in here, don't you think, Carole?"

Before Carole could answer, Veronica repeated, "Crowded? Do you think so? Then I guess you won't mind when only two other students show up at your dance in two weeks, will you?"

"As long as you're not one of them," Stevie retorted, not missing a beat. "Come on, Carole."

Veronica laughed as Stevie stormed by with Carole in tow. "An all-girls dance—now that will be really funny!" she called after them. "The boys aren't going to go, you know—not with a *tomboy* as head of the dance committee."

Stevie stopped halfway down the aisle. She turned around with her hands on her hips. She couldn't let Veronica get away with insulting her like that. What could she say that would silence her? Suddenly she had an inspiration. "It's too bad you're so down on the dance, Veronica," Stevie said clearly, emphasizing every word, "because I guess that means you don't want to be my cochairperson after all. Oh well, I'll have to find somebody else." Without giving Veronica a chance to reply, Stevie marched toward Belle's stall.

Carole followed close on her heels. "What was that all about?" she hissed.

"She's jealous, naturally."

"Of what? Explain, Stevie!"

"Sorry. I was just savoring my moment of triumph," Stevie said. At Carole's urging, she explained that Veronica had obviously found out that Miss Fenton had made Stevie head of the dance committee.

Carole congratulated Stevie on being chosen. "But you weren't really considering Veronica for the position, were you?" Carole asked as they reentered Belle's stall.

Stevie rolled her eyes. "Please, Carole! Give me some credit. I'm not completely crazy!"

"Okay, just making sure," Carole said, grinning.

Stevie glanced at her watch. "Oh no! It's almost five, and I've got to be home for dinner by five-thirty." She sighed exasperatedly. "Poor Belle. She's going to think we're *all* crazy—she's been tacked up twice, and now I don't have time to ride!"

THROUGH THE CAR window, Lisa looked out at the magnificent countryside. She'd forgotten how beautiful the truly rural part of Virginia was. Willow Creek was a pretty enough suburb, but it was no match for the acres and acres of prime hunt country she and her mother were driving through. Lisa was so captivated by the gorgeous scenery that she could almost forget the reason for her being there—almost, but not quite. The itchy kilt and stiff white blouse her mother had chosen for her to wear were a constant reminder that this trip had a purpose. *I'll bet today won't be so bad*, Lisa thought. *It is incredibly beautiful out here.* . . .

"Almost there, dear. Are you nervous?" Mrs. Atwood asked.

Startled, Lisa snapped out of her daydream. "No, Mom, why should I be nervous?" she said.

"Oh, I don't know—I always get nervous before an interview," Mrs. Atwood said.

"But Mom, it's not as if this interview really matters," Lisa said.

"You wouldn't want to make a bad impression," Mrs. Atwood said quickly. She turned to Lisa and smiled. "But I know you won't, dear. You'll do your father and me proud, the way you always do."

Lisa sighed. Her mother was constantly encouraging her to make a good impression. Even when she did an errand, she was supposed to look nice—as if the man at the grocery store cared what she was wearing! And now she was supposed to impress some interviewer she would never see again. Boy, would Stevie have laughed at that. "I'll try, Mom," Lisa said finally. *For your sake*, she added to herself.

"Good girl," Mrs. Atwood responded. "After all, you never know what can happen."

Lisa decided to ignore her mother's comment. She had no idea what it was supposed to mean, but it was pointless to argue. If her mother wanted to have dreams about sending her daughter to Wentworth, let her. Besides, just then Mrs. Atwood turned off the main road, and Lisa was more interested in finally seeing the famous Wentworth than quarreling about her chances of going there. After driving up a long, winding road bordered by stately elm trees, they pulled up to the school.

While her mother checked her hair and makeup in the rearview mirror, Lisa got out of the car. She looked around, her eyes wide. Wentworth Manor was truly something to behold. They had parked next to a formidable brick building with white columns. Beyond it were two smaller buildings in a similar style. In the distance Lisa could make out a large, rambling stable and green, rolling pastures dotted with horses.

"Boy, it looks like the set of *Gone With the Wind*," she breathed.

"I knew you'd like it!" Mrs. Atwood exclaimed, beaming.

"Mom, not so fast. I haven't even—" Before Lisa could finish, a loud bell sounded. Lisa wasn't surprised to hear it because her mother had explained that Wentworth had a half day of classes on Saturday. But she was surprised when the doors of the brick building swung open and the crowd of girls came out. They were all dressed identically, in dark green blazers, green-and-blue skirts, and knee socks and loafers.

"They have to wear uniforms?" Lisa asked, recoiling at the thought of having to wear the same thing every day.

"Yes, isn't it wonderful?" Mrs. Atwood responded eagerly. "It makes them look so ladylike. Now, come, we don't want to be late for our tour."

Reluctantly Lisa followed her mother up the stairs and into the main building, trying to ignore the eyes she felt on her back. Most of the girls looked her over curiously and then looked away, but a few stared at her. Lisa suddenly felt awkward. She kept her eyes focused downward as her mother stopped and asked a teacher where they should go for their tour. The teacher pointed down the hallway to a door marked ADMISSIONS OFFICE.

Inside the office another mother-and-daughter pair were sitting on a couch, waiting. Both were elegantly dressed, and for some reason Lisa felt more self-conscious than ever. She tried to catch the girl's eye to see if she felt as awkward as Lisa did, but the girl was reading a fashion magazine and didn't look up.

Mrs. Atwood introduced herself to the receptionist. "Wait right here," the woman replied. "I'll be back with someone to take you around in a moment."

"Isn't this exciting, Lisa? Don't the girls look nice?" Mrs. Atwood whispered.

Lisa nodded, trying to feign enthusiasm. *Nice* wasn't

the word she would have used to describe the girls who had passed them in the hallway. *Sophisticated*, maybe, or *stuck-up*—but not *nice*.

"Here we are," said the woman, returning with a student in tow. "This is Sally Whitmore. She'll be your tour guide this afternoon. Feel free to ask her any questions about Wentworth. When you get back, Mrs. Cushing will interview Lisa."

"How do you do, Mrs. Atwood? Lisa? It's very nice to meet you," the girl said, extending a manicured hand and smiling brightly.

First Mrs. Atwood, then Lisa shook hands with her. Her hand was limp, Lisa noticed—definitely not the firm handshake Max taught them to use when they were meeting new people at Pony Club rallies.

As Sally headed them down a hallway, Lisa gave her a sidelong glance. She had long blond hair and looked a few years older than Lisa. Lisa could tell that her mother was pleased with Sally's good manners, but Lisa wasn't so easily persuaded. She knew it was important to shake hands, but there was something about the girl's smile she didn't buy. It looked fake, instead of truly warm and welcoming. It reminded her of someone else's smile. Of course: Veronica diAngelo's!

"I'm sure you'll be interested in seeing this, Lisa,"

Sally was saying. "It's the student center, and it's just been renovated."

Lisa peered in at the nearly empty room.

"Isn't it nice, dear?" Mrs. Atwood said anxiously.

"Yeah, it's great, Mom," Lisa replied, keeping her real thoughts to herself. The student center, a large room with couches, tables, and magazines, did look okay. It just seemed strange that hardly anyone was hanging out there. At Lisa's school, the student lounge was always packed. And even though Lisa tried to avoid it when it was full of obnoxious boys, she liked the communal spirit of the place. The Wentworth student center was so deserted and quiet, it might as well have been the library.

The tour went on, and Lisa found herself comparing Wentworth again and again to Willow Creek Junior High. To be fair, Wentworth definitely had some pluses. The classrooms were spacious and quiet, with views of the surrounding countryside. The computer room had twenty computers that looked brand new. And the theater was incredible—it was in a separate building and looked almost professional. Even though the stage at Willow Creek had been improved over the years, it was now run-down and in desperate need of refurbishing. But despite how nice the Wentworth facility was, something didn't feel right to Lisa. She wondered what it was as she followed Sally and her mother from building to building.

Near the end of the tour she realized the problem: The whole school was like the student center—too quiet. It felt more like a hospital than a school. Nobody was calling out or banging lockers or bustling around. Instead, uniformed girls walked in groups of twos and threes, chatting quietly. Lisa tried to tell herself that Willow Creek would have been a lot quieter without the boys—and especially the obnoxious boys—but still, the lack of noise gave her the creeps. And trying to come up with appropriate responses to her mother's and Sally's promptings was tiring. Lisa was almost glad when the tour ended and Sally dropped them back at the admissions office.

"Do you have any questions?" Sally asked.

"I can't think of a single one. You answered them all so thoroughly on the tour," Mrs. Atwood gushed. "Lisa?"

"Nope," Lisa said. "The tour was great," she added so that she wouldn't sound so abrupt. The truth was, she did have some questions, but she wasn't sure Sally Whitmore was the right person to answer them. She didn't look like the kind of person Lisa could ask, "So, what do you do for fun around here?"

After making sure they were resettled in the office, Sally left, promising to pick Lisa up in an hour to take her to see the barn. A few minutes later Mrs. Cushing, the director of admissions, emerged from her office. She was a tall, slim woman, dressed in a tweed suit, with her hair pulled back in a severe bun. Before taking Lisa in for her interview, she drew Mrs. Atwood aside for a moment. Lisa strained her ears but, to her annoyance, couldn't hear anything they said. Then it was Lisa's turn.

"I'll see you in a while, dear," Mrs. Atwood said, leaning over to give Lisa a quick kiss. "Good luck!" she whispered into Lisa's ear. "Knock 'em dead!"

To her surprise, Lisa felt sad to see her mother go, even for a short time. But she gritted her teeth. Soon the whole Wentworth episode would be over and she would never have to think about the school again. Her mother was going to drive into the town of Richfield and look around. Then she would come back to pick Lisa up.

The interview seemed to speed by. Lisa could hardly believe how little Mrs. Cushing asked her. Instead of making her answer questions, the woman spent most of the hour telling her what a privilege it was to go to Wentworth. "You do realize that we have girls from the best families in the Northeast and the South here at Wentworth, don't you, Ms. Atwood?" she asked.

Lisa nodded uncertainly, not sure what Mrs. Cushing meant by *best*.

"We have over ten applicants for *every spot*. Getting

in is extremely competitive," Mrs. Cushing went on, frowning across her massive desk.

"And once a girl comes here, we expect her to be a credit to the school in *every way*. And we expect her to behave, Ms. Atwood. We're not like some boarding schools who let their girls run wild. Oh, no—that's not the Wentworth way. If a girl gets in trouble, she can be sent home—"

"I don't think I—" Lisa started to say.

"For good!" Mrs. Cushing thundered. "With no chance of readmission."

"I see. I—"

"Ever! Once you're out, you're out. And that's final. All right?"

Lisa nodded. "Good," said Mrs. Cushing briskly. "I'm glad we understand one another."

At that, Lisa had to stifle a grin. She had never understood anyone less than she understood Mrs. Cushing at that moment. She had no idea what the woman was talking about. And Mrs. Cushing clearly didn't understand her. Lisa never got into trouble at school. She never acted up, she never talked back—for heaven's sakes, she'd been tardy only a few times in her life. Yet Mrs. Cushing was actually lecturing her on her behavior! When Stevie and Carole heard that, they would die laughing.

Mrs. Cushing also didn't seem to understand that this was just an interview—she was acting as if Lisa were going to enroll at Wentworth that minute. Lisa didn't understand *why* Mrs. Cushing didn't understand. Surely her mother must have explained their financial situation to the headmistress.

Lisa didn't have time to ponder the matter further. Before she knew it, she was shaking Mrs. Cushing's hand and Sally was back to take her to the stables. It was a beautiful Virginia fall day. As the two girls walked toward the barn, Lisa relaxed. "How long have you been riding?" she asked Sally, hoping to start a friendly conversation.

"Not very long," said the older girl. "I'm not good at all compared to some of the other girls, like Beth Reynolds or Ashley Briggs."

Lisa noticed Sally sounded defensive. "I know how that is," she said. "My two best friends have been riding practically since they could walk, so I always feel like a beginner compared to them."

"Oh, I don't feel like a beginner," Sally said scornfully. "I've taken Cotton Socks to tons of A shows."

"Oh, really?" Lisa said, unable to keep a hint of doubt out of her voice. So much for sympathy. If Sally had gone to so many A shows, why did she have to brag about them?

43

"Yes, haven't you?" Sally asked.

"No, but I'm very involved in Pony Club," Lisa said, knowing she sounded defensive now, too.

"That's nice," Sally said with forced politeness.

The two of them walked the rest of the way to the stables in silence, but once inside the barn, Lisa was unable to contain her enthusiasm. "It's beautiful!" she exclaimed, gazing down a long aisle of stalls.

"We like it," Sally said coolly.

Lisa walked slowly down the aisle, feasting her eyes on the fine Thoroughbred heads that looked out at her. Every stall had a large brass nameplate on it with its inhabitant's name and the owner's name below that. Matching blue-and-green Wentworth blankets hung over the doors. The stalls themselves were huge and immaculate. In fact, it was one of the cleanest barns Lisa had ever seen. There was hardly a wisp of hay anywhere. After she had taken her stroll down the aisle, Lisa rejoined Sally, who was waiting at the entrance with a bored expression.

"Where's the tack room?" Lisa asked, eager to have a look at it.

"It's one aisle over," Sally replied. "But why would you want to see that? We never use it."

"You mean someone cleans your tack for you?"

Lisa asked, realizing the implications of what Sally had said.

"Of course," Sally said. "You don't think we have time for that, do you? Wentworth is very rigorous academically, you know."

"Right," Lisa said. So much for making friendly conversation. She took one more stab at it. "Well, in that case, I'd love to meet your horse," she said.

"Cotton? Oh, I don't know where he is now. He could be turned out or being exercised. Who knows? So, do you want to see the indoor ring? It's one of the biggest in the state."

"Why not?" Lisa said. The truth was, she'd suddenly gotten a perfect picture of what riding was like at Wentworth, and she didn't really care if she saw anything else. But she still had time to kill before her mother came, so she followed Sally out of the barn and into the spectator seats of the huge ring.

A number of girls were riding. That struck Lisa as strange, since it was such a nice day. "Isn't there an outside ring?" she asked Sally.

"Sure, but it's too much of a pain to get to. It's a five-minute ride," Sally said.

Just then one of the girls riding shrieked. As Lisa watched, the girl spun her horse around and galloped pell-mell toward them. Right before she got to the side of the ring, she stood up in her stirrups, hauled on the reins, and jerked the horse to a stop. "Sally! What's up?" she cried.

"Ashley! This is Lisa Atwood from Willow Creek. She rides, so she wanted to see the stables," Sally said. She sounded more enthusiastic than she'd been all afternoon.

"Willow Creek? You're kidding! I used to live there!" Ashley cried. "Back when I was little. Boring, isn't it? But at least you can ride there. So, where do you keep your horse, Lisa?"

"I—I don't have my own horse," Lisa said uncomfortably.

Ashley and Sally looked at her. "You don't?" they said in unison.

"No, I ride one at the stable where I take lessons," Lisa said. "At Pine Hollow," she added.

"At least the stable's decent," Ashley said. "You probably know Veronica diAngelo. She's one of my best friends."

"Yes, I know her," Lisa said. *Boy, do I know her,* she thought.

"Buster, stop it!" Ashley barked, jerking on the reins again. Lisa didn't know what, exactly, Ashley wanted Buster to stop. The beautiful black hunter had merely

46

shifted his weight from side to side. He was restless, the way all horses were when they were suddenly halted and asked to stand still.

"You'd get a horse if you came to Wentworth, though, wouldn't you?" Sally asked.

"I guess so," Lisa said. Sally's "if you came to Wentworth" was so impossible to imagine that Lisa figured she might as well say whatever she felt like.

"Well, if you're in the market, you can buy Buster here—cheap," Ashley said, laughing at her own joke. She took her jumping bat and drummed the horse between the ears a couple of times. Buster jerked his head up and laid his ears back. "See how bad-tempered he is? Aren't you, you stupid horse?"

Lisa clenched her hands and forced herself to breathe calmly. What she wanted to do was drag Ashley to the ground and rub her face in the dirt for being so unfair to her horse.

"All right, Ash, we'd better go. Lisa's mother will be waiting for her," Sally said.

"Okay, but promise me you'll come to my room tonight so we can redo our manicures," Ashley said.

"Right after dinner," Sally promised.

"Great. Nice to meet you, Lisa. Tell Ronnie I said hi and I miss her loads, and I'm going to come visit her soon, okay?"

47

"Sure," Lisa said, smiling, "the next time I speak to her." *Which hopefully will be about a decade from now*, she added silently.

With a wave of her hand, Ashley spurred Buster into a trot and rode off.

"So you know one of Ashley's old friends?" Sally asked on the way back, obviously impressed.

"Oh yes," Lisa said, "Veronica and I go way back." *Maybe not as friends*, she thought, *but we do go way back*.

The fact that Ashley and Lisa knew someone in common seemed to have raised Lisa's status immeasurably in Sally's sight. All at once Sally was friendly and talkative. She kept up a steady stream of conversation on the way to the parking lot, where Mrs. Atwood was waiting. When Lisa thanked her for the tour of the stables, Sally protested, "Oh, don't thank me! It was my pleasure. As you can see, Wentworth is a great school, and I'm just glad to do my part to show it off. If you have any questions, please call me. You too, Mrs. Atwood," she added.

"Thank you, Sally. I'm sure Lisa will want to talk to you some more," said Mrs. Atwood.

Lisa stood by the car door holding her breath and counting the seconds until she could kiss Wentworth good-bye forever. Finally—*finally*—her mother finished thanking Sally for the millionth time, and got into the car.

As soon as they were heading down the driveway, Lisa let out a huge sigh of relief. She had done her part. She had tried to make a good impression. She had kept her mouth shut when she couldn't think of anything good to say. And now the whole ordeal was over. Her mother would forget all about Wentworth in a few days and find something else she wanted Lisa to try. As for Lisa, she couldn't wait to get back to Pine Hollow and find out what she had missed.

"So, tell me all about it! How were the stables?" Mrs. Atwood asked.

"Fine, Mom," Lisa said exhaustedly.

"Just fine? I thought they were supposed to be top-notch."

"They are top-notch. They're beautiful, Mom," Lisa said.

"So you liked the school?" Mrs. Atwood asked.

Lisa closed her eyes, wishing her mother would stop asking her questions. If she told her mother the truth, she'd be in for a two-hour lecture, all the way home, about how great Wentworth was and what a privilege it would be to go there. Instead she said with a sigh, "Yeah, Mom. It was nice." There. That ought to be enough to get her to drop the subject.

Lisa hurried over to Pine Hollow early Sunday morning. For some reason she hadn't felt like calling Stevie and Carole the night before. By the time she'd gotten home, she'd been so fed up with seeing Wentworth and then hearing her mother talk about it in the car that she just couldn't gear up to repeat the whole story for them. But after a good night's sleep, she felt de-Wentworthed and back to her old self. She couldn't wait to see Carole and Stevie.

Luckily they'd had the same idea. As Lisa entered the stable, Carole came around a corner carrying a saddle, and Stevie ducked out of Belle's stall.

"I guess great minds think alike," Stevie said.

"I was hoping you'd both be here," Lisa said, pleased that she'd guessed right.

"And I was hoping all three of you would be here," a voice said behind them. The girls turned to greet Mrs. Reg, who was carrying a bucketful of new salt blocks. "Listen, girls. I've got to distribute the rest of these, so how about sweeping out the tack room for me and tidying it up before you ride? It could really use it."

The girls were eager to comply. Cleaning the tack room was a perfect task for The Saddle Club because they could talk while they worked. A few minutes later Stevie and Lisa were lugging tack trunks and sawhorses out of the room so that Carole could get busy with the broom. Stevie was dying to ask Lisa about Wentworth, but she held back, remembering Carole's suggestion that Lisa might not want to discuss it.

Finally Lisa said teasingly, "So, aren't you going to ask me about it?"

"What did you think?" Stevie blurted out.

"That depends," Lisa said, her eyes twinkling. "What did I think of *it*, or what did I think of *them*? *It* is a beautiful school with the most gorgeous stables I've ever seen."

"And them?" Stevie asked.

"They're horrible!" said Lisa. "All I could think the

whole time I was there was that if this is how being rich makes you, I *never* want to have a lot of money."

"So the girls weren't nice?" Carole asked, pausing with the broom in her hand.

"I only really met two of them," Lisa said, "but that was two too many!" She told Carole and Stevie about Sally Whitmore and Ashley Briggs, how rude they were, and how it was clear that neither of them gave a darn about their horses.

"Ashley Briggs—that's the girl I was telling you about, Carole. She's Veronica's friend," Stevie explained.

Lisa nodded. "Yes, she told me she used to live here. I'm supposed to say hi to 'Ronnie' for her," she said sarcastically.

"Well, here's your chance," Carole murmured, nodding toward the door.

The three of them fell silent as Veronica entered the room. "Don't mind me," Veronica said, "I'm just here to grab a pitchfork."

"A pitchfork?" Carole asked. "But—why?" She didn't mean to be rude, but Veronica's asking for a pitchfork was shocking. She never, ever mucked out stalls or cleaned up after her horse.

"Yes, a pitchfork, Carole. On my way in, I noticed that Belle's stall was a little messy, and I was going to do Stevie a favor and get the worst of it out."

"You *were?*" Stevie said, agog.

"You *were?*" Carole and Lisa repeated.

"Sure, why not? Hard work doesn't bother me," Veronica said, to the amazement of The Saddle Club. "Now, where's that pitchfork?"

Stevie, Lisa, and Carole were so startled that it took them a minute to focus on what Veronica was asking. There was a long silence. "Veronica, the pitchforks and shovels aren't kept in the tack room," Lisa finally said.

"They're not?" Veronica said, her face falling.

"No. They're hanging in the empty stall at the end of the aisle."

"Oh. Right." There was another awkward pause.

To break the silence, Lisa said, "Say, Veronica, I met a friend of yours yesterday—Ashley Briggs. She says hello." Lisa figured that was sufficient—she didn't particularly want to add the part about Ashley's missing Veronica "loads" and wanting to come visit.

"Where on earth would *you* have met Ashley?" Veronica asked, startled into dropping her polite act.

"Actually," Lisa said, relishing the fact for a fleeting second, "I was interviewing at Wentworth Manor."

"You?" Veronica cried. "*You* were interviewing at Wentworth? I can't believe it! Why would *you* interview there?" Her dark eyes flashed angrily.

"My mother wanted me to," Lisa said simply.

"*Your* mother! That's the most ridiculous thing I've ever heard!" Veronica shrieked. She turned on her heel and stomped out of the tack room.

"Could someone translate that for me?" Carole asked, unable to make sense of the scene she had just witnessed. Veronica had gone from ingratiating sweetness to openly raging hostility in a matter of seconds.

"I'm pretty sure I can," Stevie said. "Let's finish up here and then go somewhere far away from her."

"How about we take a nice long trail ride?" Lisa suggested. After being gone a day, she couldn't wait to tack up Prancer and go for a ride.

"Good idea. Starlight needs to stretch his legs after all that drilling we did in Horse Wise," Carole said. "And as a matter of fact, so do I."

"Oh, how was the lesson?" Lisa asked. As they finished sweeping and tidying the tack room, Carole and Stevie filled Lisa in on yesterday's Pony Club mounted meeting. Max had made them ride without stirrups through a series of dressage movements for most of the hour. It had been intense work that required high concentration on the part of horse and rider. A trail ride would be just the right change for today.

Working quickly, the girls had the tack room clean and the horses groomed and saddled within half an hour. They mounted up and set off at a leisurely pace, letting

Starlight, Prancer, and Belle walk on loose reins. As soon as the trail was wide enough for them to bunch up, Stevie turned eagerly in her saddle. "Now, where should I start? Which do you want to know first: why Veronica was being nice or why she freaked out?"

"I'll bet I know why she was so nice at the beginning," Carole ventured. "The dance, right?"

"Exactly," Stevie said. "She heard that I haven't picked a cochairperson of the dance committee. Yesterday, after Horse Wise, she was hinting that I should choose her, so I hinted back that first I would need to make sure she's capable of hard work. I didn't think she'd actually take the bait, but it looks like I was wrong."

"It sure does. At least, she's definitely working hard to get on your good side," Carole commented.

"What dance committee, Stevie?" Lisa asked, her interest piqued. Anything that involved Veronica's having to kowtow to The Saddle Club was sure to be good for a few laughs.

Briefly Stevie recounted her meeting Friday afternoon with Miss Fenton and her subsequent run-in with Veronica. "I got so mad at Veronica for insulting *my* dance that I pretended I'd been considering her for my cochair," Stevie concluded.

"So, now she's trying to get you to change your mind, huh?" said Lisa.

"Yes, and I must say that I look forward to watching her try—and try and try and try," Stevie said devilishly.

"Why not? It will be good for Pine Hollow. She's already learned where the pitchforks are kept," Carole said with a laugh. "That's a lot for her to absorb in one day."

After walking for a while, the girls came to a grassy verge, and the horses began to pull on their bits, asking to go faster. Without further ado, Stevie challenged, "Race you to the top?" Not bothering to wait for an answer, she leaned forward over Belle's neck and urged the mare forward. Carole and Lisa followed suit, and the three of them galloped up the small hill. Prancer beat the other two by a neck.

"We win in a photo finish!" Lisa cried, slowing the mare to a trot and then a walk.

"No fair riding an ex-racehorse!" Stevie called back.

Lisa grinned. "At Wentworth, they couldn't believe that I don't own a horse."

"That's because they all have five or six horses each. They bring a different one to school every semester," Stevie said.

"Really, Stevie?" Carole asked, bringing Starlight in line with the other two.

"Okay, maybe not every semester, but I've heard of

girls there doing badly at a show and then calling Daddy to collect one horse and send another."

"Boy, Veronica would fit in perfectly there," Carole said. Veronica was known for blaming all her mistakes on whichever horse she happened to be riding.

"Actually, Carole, you're almost right," Stevie began mischievously. "But instead of fitting *in* at Wentworth, Veronica *had* a fit."

"Huh? You mean Veronica used to go to Wentworth?" Lisa asked.

"Correction: She *wanted* to go to Wentworth; she *tried* to go to Wentworth—"

"But?" said Lisa.

"But Wentworth wouldn't have her," Stevie replied. "I can't believe I didn't remember this before, but Veronica looked at Wentworth once, too."

"She interviewed there?" Lisa asked.

"Interviewed there, took the tour—the works."

"So what happened? I would have thought her parents could have gotten her in," Lisa said. Mr. diAngelo was a prominent banker and reputed to be the richest man in Willow Creek—just the kind of person Mrs. Cushing would love to brag about, Lisa guessed.

"Naturally," Stevie said. "And I'm sure they would have. Except for one teeny little incident: Veronica got into a screaming fight with her mother right in the admissions office."

"You're kidding," Lisa said, grinning.

"Nope. She got so mad, she threw a vase across the room," Stevie said gleefully.

"Did it smash?" Carole asked.

"It smashed all right," said Stevie. "It hit the floor right as the director of admissions was coming out to meet the diAngelos."

"You mean Mrs. Cushing?" Lisa asked, imagining the outraged expression on the older woman's face.

"I think that was her name," Stevie said. "The story was the best gossip in the Fenton Hall Parents' Association for months."

"Wow," Lisa breathed, "Veronica versus her mother and Mrs. Cushing."

"Yup," Stevie said. "So now the diAngelos hate Wentworth Manor. If you want to see Mrs. diAngelo turn purple, just mention that school."

"But if they hate it so much, why would Veronica care if Lisa's applying?" Carole asked.

"Well, they do hate it, but it's more complicated than that. Kind of what you'd call a love-hate relationship," Stevie mused, warming to her subject. "The way I look at it is like this: The diAngelos know that Wentworth is

58

one of the snobbiest schools around, so they have to respect it because they love snobs, but they hate it for rejecting Veronica. And Veronica is still friends with Ashley Briggs, but she's probably really jealous of her for going there. On the other hand . . ."

Stevie had plenty more to say about the diAngelos and Wentworth Manor, and by the time she finished, the girls had arrived back at Pine Hollow. After cooling out their horses and giving them another good grooming, they reconvened in the driveway, carrying halters and lead ropes. They were going to bring in a few horses Max needed for his afternoon lesson.

Veronica was there, too, waiting for her ride home. She seemed to have regained her composure after her earlier outburst. She came over to them, smiling brightly. "Did you have a nice ride?" she asked.

"We sure did," Stevie said. "How about you? Did you take Danny out or were you too busy mucking stalls?" She couldn't keep from snickering at the thought of Veronica mucking out.

"I was too busy with the stalls," Veronica said sweetly. "Didn't you notice how nice Belle's looked?"

Stevie thought for a minute. She had noticed that it was less messy than usual when they got back, but she'd figured that Red O'Malley, Pine Hollow's stable hand, had been in there while they were gone. It was too hard to believe that Veronica had cleaned Belle's stall. "So you actually cleaned it?" Stevie said.

"Oh, it's nothing, really," Veronica said, seeming to take Stevie's comment as a thank-you. She turned suddenly to Lisa. "Did you get your hair cut, Lisa? It looks really good."

"Thanks, Veronica," Lisa said stiffly.

"No, I mean it," Veronica went on. "What salon do you go to?"

"I got it done at Cosmo Cuts," Lisa said.

Veronica looked momentarily taken aback, but she quickly recovered. "Great choice. I love that salon, and so does my mother. She and I get our hair done there every week."

"Speak of the devil . . . ," Stevie murmured, seeing Mrs. diAngelo's large white Mercedes turn onto the driveway.

"What did you say, Stevie?" Veronica asked.

"Nothing, nothing. I just said, keep up the good work—in the barn, I mean," Stevie said. She couldn't resist adding under her breath, "I'm sure I can find a lot more for you to do tomorrow."

Before hopping into her mother's car, Veronica complimented Lisa on her hair again. Then she waved goodbye to the group. "Ta-ta! See you all soon!"

The three of them watched the car disappear down the driveway. "Boy, I love it when Veronica's running scared," Stevie murmured.

"She really wants that dance job, doesn't she?" Carole asked as they headed toward the pasture where the horses were turned out.

"Sure," said Stevie. "She thinks it will boost her popularity. And now that she thinks Lisa is going to go to Wentworth Manor, she wants to get on her good side, too."

"You think so?" Lisa asked skeptically. She couldn't imagine being nice to someone just because of the school she went to.

"Definitely. She probably thinks you'll make lots of socialite friends there and look down on her," Stevie said. "Or else bad-mouth her to the other girls."

"Gee, maybe Lisa should pretend she *is* going to Wentworth," Carole suggested playfully. "Then she'll have Veronica under her thumb, too."

"Do you realize what this means?" Stevie said, looking eagerly from Carole to Lisa. "Veronica has to be nice to two of us—and for no reason at all! Because wild horses couldn't make me choose her for the dance committee."

"And wild horses couldn't drag me back to that school!" Lisa said.

6

"BYE, MRS. DOLAN!" Lisa called to her bus driver, hopping off at her stop. She swung her book bag happily as she walked toward her house. It had been a great day at school. Sometimes, Lisa realized, it took leaving a place to make you realize how much you liked it. Having spent an afternoon at Wentworth Manor, Lisa had looked at her old school with new eyes. She'd noticed all kinds of things during the day that she was normally oblivious to—like how nice Mrs. Dolan was to the kids on her bus. Even things like the beat-up lockers at Willow Creek seemed homey.

Lisa had always liked her teachers, but today she'd

appreciated them even more. As for the other kids, there were some Lisa couldn't stand, but she had lots of friends, too. The simple fact was that she belonged at Willow Creek, in a way she could never belong at Wentworth. In a sense, her mother was right: Interviewing at Wentworth had been a privilege—it had made her realize how privileged she already was.

Before going into the house, Lisa stopped to get the mail, as she always did. She flipped quickly through the pile of letters but didn't see anything interesting—no foreign stamps meaning a card from the Italian boys The Saddle Club knew; no Los Angeles postmark indicating a letter from Skye Ransom, their movie star friend, who lived out in Beverly Hills.

"Mom, I'm home!" Lisa called, stopping in the kitchen to drop off the mail and grab an apple. She glanced at the clock above the kitchen table. She had just enough time to grab her riding clothes and walk to Pine Hollow. She didn't want to miss watching Veronica do any of the tasks Stevie was going to think up for her. It was too funny to see Veronica doing actual work.

Lisa dashed upstairs to her room and was pulling her hair into a ponytail when she heard her mother cry out from the kitchen. She ran to the head of the stairs. "Are you okay, Mom?" she called.

"I'm—I'm fine!" Mrs. Atwood called back. "I'm just

63

shaken up. I can't believe it! Oh, honey, it's too good to be true!"

"What? What is it, Mom?" Lisa cried, running downstairs.

Her mother was sitting at the kitchen table, an open Express Mail letter in her hand. She looked completely overcome with happiness, as if she might cry. "Mom?" Lisa asked gently.

Mrs. Atwood looked up at her. "It's everything we've ever hoped for, darling," she said, her voice trembling. "You got a full scholarship, Lisa. You're going to Wentworth!"


"No, I'M SORRY, Veronica," Stevie said. "I just haven't made my decision yet."

"But—" Veronica began.

Stevie held up a hand. "You can understand how I feel. A lot of people are begging me for the job, and I have to be fair," she said in her best teacherly manner.

"But shouldn't you decide soon? The dance is less than two weeks away," Veronica said anxiously.

"Hmmm . . . Yes, I guess you're right. I'll tell you what: I'll definitely make the announcement by Friday, okay?"

"Friday?" Veronica said, her face falling.

"Now, now. Chin up, Veronica. Look on the bright

side: You've got a whole week to impress me. Listen, why don't you make a list of possible themes for the dance, and submit it to me in school tomorrow," Stevie said. She watched Veronica to see how she would react, sure that Veronica would tell her to shove it.

A look of annoyance flickered over Veronica's face, but she said nothing, just nodded, turned on her heel, and headed off toward Danny's stall.

Stevie grinned wickedly. "You don't have to type it— handwritten is fine, as long as it's neat," she called after Veronica.

Emerging from the tack room, Carole noticed the look of devilish delight on Stevie's face. "All right. What have you got her doing now?" she asked.

"Carole, please. I don't *have* her doing anything. It's all strictly voluntary. Veronica *wanted* to show me some sample decorations made out of hay and corn. And is it my fault that she insisted on coming here right after school and grooming Belle for me? Can I *help* it if she's trying to be my friend?" Stevie asked innocently.

Carole shook her head, laughing. If Stevie had been tormenting anyone else this way, she would have warned the person immediately. But Veronica deserved it. Besides, it was good for Veronica to do some barn work for a change. Normally she was waited on hand and foot.

"If Belle's all groomed, how about helping me with Starlight?" Carole said.

Stevie was happy to comply. The two girls brushed the gelding's bay coat till it gleamed. "Maybe we should start on Prancer, too. Lisa must be running late today," Stevie said when Carole was going over Starlight with a rub rag.

Carole glanced at her watch. "That's funny. I saw her outside after school, and she said she was just going home to change and then coming right over."

"Mrs. Atwood probably signed her up for Monday-afternoon embroidery lessons," Stevie joked.

"It would hardly surprise me," Carole said ruefully. "She sure has some strange ideas."

"I know," Stevie agreed. "Can you imagine Lisa at Wentworth Manor? The girls aren't smart at all. They'd have to let her skip about three grades."

"If they're not smart, how do they get in?" Carole asked. The boarding-school concept still mystified her.

"Probably family connections. They know the 'right' people or else their parents donate a lot of money," Stevie said. "Doesn't it make you sick?"

"If Lisa cared about getting in, it would," Carole said, picking a few shavings out of Starlight's tail. "But since she'd never want to go there, maybe it's good that her parents aren't well-connected—whatever that means."

66

"Good point," Stevie said. "Then Mrs. Atwood would really be out of control."

Carole nodded. "You're right about that. I'm just glad for Lisa's sake that her trip to Wentworth is over. I think it was worrying her more than she admitted."

"Heck, I'd be stressed if I had to go within ten miles of that place for any reason other than riding. Those Worth-a-lot girls are horrible."

"I guess they're Went-worthless," Carole said, and giggled.

Leaving Starlight cross-tied, the two of them took Prancer out of her stall and gave her a quick once-over. Twenty minutes later, when they had tacked up their own horses, Lisa still hadn't arrived.

"Boy, this is getting to be a habit," Stevie said.

"What is?" Carole asked.

"Grooming a horse for one of us who's absent, and then the person never coming."

Carole nodded thoughtfully. Today she couldn't imagine what had gotten into Lisa. "Oh well. I guess we can ride by ourselves."

"Sure, but her excuse had better be good," Stevie said with mock severity.

They put Prancer back in her stall and mounted near the good-luck horseshoe. The horseshoe was a tradition at Pine Hollow. All the riders touched it before setting off on a ride. No rider had ever been seriously injured at the stables. "Remind me to tell Veronica to give the horseshoe a polish," Stevie said once she was aboard Belle. "It's looking a little tarnished, wouldn't you say?"

Carole grinned. "Just a touch, yes." Feeling Starlight begin to dance, she sat deeply in the saddle to steady him. Like many well-bred horses, Starlight could be high-strung at times. It took a confident rider to keep him in line. "Why don't we work in the indoor ring?" Carole suggested. "Starlight's feeling his oats today, and that way, when Lisa comes, she'll be able to find us right away."

Stevie agreed. On their way in, she said jokingly to Carole, "Maybe she's not coming, though. Maybe she decided to go to Wentworth after all."

Carole gave her a withering glance. "Yeah, right," she said. "In a wagon pulled by wild horses."

LISA LAY ON her bed, staring at the ceiling. *You got a full scholarship. . . . You're going to Wentworth. . . . You got a full scholarship. . . . It's everything we've ever hoped for. . . . It's everything we've ever hoped for. . . . You're going to Wentworth. . . .* Like a bad song on the radio, her mother's words had been repeating in her head all afternoon. She still couldn't quite believe them, though. Was she really going to leave home and go to that school with those awful girls?

"Lisa! Your father's home! Time for dinner!" Mrs. Atwood called.

Lisa sat up with a start. She'd been lying there for

almost three hours. She'd forgotten all about going to Pine Hollow. After telling her the news, Lisa's mother had decided to run out to the grocery store and buy food for a celebratory dinner. Lisa had come up to her room and had hardly moved for the rest of the afternoon. The only thing that gave her a spark of hope was the time of year. Since the semesters were under way at both Wentworth and Willow Creek, she probably wouldn't be switching schools until at least January. Maybe somehow by then she could figure something out . . .

"Did you have a good nap, honey?" her mother asked as Lisa sat down at the table. "I hated to wake you, but I figured you'd be hungry. And I made fried chicken and mashed potatoes, your favorite—even though I'm breaking my diet."

Lisa did her best to smile, but it was difficult. "I wasn't taking a nap, Mom."

"Really? Just letting the news sink in, hmm? Isn't it exciting?" her mother asked.

Lisa nodded wordlessly.

Lisa's father came in, freshly changed out of his suit. Mr. Atwood tended to be a quiet, serious person. Rather than exclaim excitedly, as her mother had done, he said somberly, "Congratulations, Lisa. We're so proud of you." But Lisa could tell that the news had made him very happy.

"It's nothing, Dad," she responded. "I didn't do anything. I didn't even know I was being considered for a scholarship."

"That's right, honey," said Mrs. Atwood, joining them at the table. "I didn't want to get your hopes up in case you didn't get it. I also didn't want to interfere if you didn't like the school. But then when you said how nice you thought Wentworth was, I started to hope like crazy."

Lisa frowned, not quite understanding. Why did her mother think she liked Wentworth?

"Imagine the opportunities you'll have," Mrs. Atwood continued. "You'll meet girls from everywhere—diplomats' children, Washington socialites, probably even movie stars' daughters, for all I know. Now, eat up, dear, don't let it get cold."

Lisa stared at the chicken and mashed potatoes. For some reason her favorite meal looked distinctly unappetizing. Of course, she wouldn't say anything to her mother about it. She wouldn't want to— All of a sudden, Lisa felt a chill run through her. She looked up at her mother, barely hearing what she was saying. She knew why her mother thought she liked Wentworth. She had *told* her she did! She had said she thought it was "really nice" and had kept her true feelings to herself! She hadn't wanted to disappoint her mother, who had

71

worked so hard to get her the interview, who cared so much about being socially correct. Of course, Lisa had never dreamed that there was even the slightest risk in not telling her mother the truth. But she hadn't counted on a full scholarship.

It all made sense, too, based on what Stevie had said about the girls at Wentworth. Stevie had said they weren't smart—only rich. So the school probably loved to find girls like Lisa who could boost its academic ranking. Lisa wasn't stuck-up, but she knew she was smarter than Ashley Briggs and Sally Whitmore.

"Honey? Lisa?"

Lisa snapped to attention. "What did you say, Mom?"

"I was just asking if you had told Carole and Stevie the good news. I'm sure they'll be very proud to have a good friend at a school like Wentworth. And going to Wentworth will do wonders for your riding. Did you already tell them how nice the stables were?"

"No, Mom, not yet," Lisa said quietly, a new wave of dread washing over her. How could she tell Carole and Stevie? They would never understand. If she went to boarding school, what would become of The Saddle Club? Would the two of them keep on having it without her?

"Lisa, are you all right?" Mr. Atwood asked gently. "You look a bit pale."

"I'm fine, Dad. I guess it's just the shock of the news. I can't seem to take it all in. . . ." Lisa let her voice trail off. Both of her parents were looking anxiously at her. She didn't know what to say.

"I'm sure it's quite overwhelming," her mother finally said. "Think of all of the prominent people in Willow Creek who will sit up and take notice when they hear that Lisa Atwood is going to Wentworth Manor."

Mr. Atwood leaned over and patted Lisa reassuringly on the shoulder. "But the most important thing is that you're happy, sweetheart," he reminded her.

"Well, of course!" Mrs. Atwood said emphatically. "And we'll miss you very, very much. You do know that, don't you, Lisa?"

Lisa nodded, not trusting herself to speak. She had hardly even thought about the part of boarding school that meant leaving her parents, she'd been so caught up in how horrible the Wentworth girls had been. Now Wentworth looked bad in yet another way.

Somehow Lisa managed to eat a few bites of her dinner and help clear the table. As she and her father were bringing the dishes to the sink, Lisa asked, "So, when will I be starting, Mom?"

Mrs. Atwood paused, turning from the fridge. "Why, right away. Didn't I tell you?"

"Right away?" Lisa cried. "What do you mean? Tomorrow?"

"Oh no. We've got too much to do for you to leave tomorrow. I spoke with Mrs. Cushing on the phone today, and I arranged for you to start in two weeks. It's a little unusual for them to accept a new student after classes have started, but she was so impressed with your school record that they're making an exception. And she knew your father and I didn't find out about the scholarship application until late in the summer. So we'll have to run errands all week to get you ready. You'd better tell your teachers tomorrow."

After "two weeks," Lisa hardly heard anything her mother said. In *two weeks* she was going to be going to school at Wentworth Manor? And living there? "Mom, do you mind if I go up to my room?" Lisa said. She felt suddenly weak.

"No, of course not, dear. You're sure you're okay?" Mrs. Atwood asked. She put a hand on Lisa's forehead. "You don't feel hot. It must be all the excitement. Why don't you go to bed early?"

UP IN HER ROOM, Lisa sat on her pink bed and stared at the phone. She had to call Carole and Stevie and tell them. But how could she begin? Slowly she dialed Stevie's number, then waited while Stevie, who had three-way calling, dialed Carole. Once they were all on the line, Lisa somehow found her voice and started to talk. "I called because I have to tell you guys something," she began.

"Good, because we have to update you on Veronica's attempts to be made cochair of the dance committee," Stevie said eagerly, settling back in her chair for a long conversation. When a Saddle Club member missed even one day at Pine Hollow, it always seemed as if there was a lot of catching up to do. "So, what's your news?" she prompted Lisa.

"Yeah, Lis', where were you today?" Carole asked.

Fighting to hold back tears, Lisa blurted out, "You guys, it's serious."

In their own rooms, Carole and Stevie listened with extra attention. From the tone of Lisa's voice, they could tell that she wasn't in the mood for the usual joking banter the three of them got into on the telephone. "Lisa, what is it?" Carole asked.

"I'm going to Wentworth," Lisa said, dropping the bomb the only way she knew how. "I leave in two weeks."

There was a long, long silence. Stevie thought for a second that maybe Lisa was putting them on, but she knew practical jokes weren't Lisa's style. Besides, her voice sounded too shaky for her to be making it up.

"You mean your parents are sending you?" Carole asked. She didn't want to come right out and ask about the money, but she was confused. Lisa had said, and Stevie had confirmed, that her parents would never be able to afford the Wentworth tuition.

"Yes, they're sending me, but they don't have to pay. I—I got a scholarship," Lisa said.

"A scholarship!" Stevie exclaimed, horrified. "Of course! Why didn't I think of that? They'd be dying to give a scholarship to someone like you, Lisa. But that doesn't mean you have to take it, you know."

"It does as far as my parents are concerned," Lisa said, hearing an edge creep into her voice.

"Why? Can't you talk to them?" Stevie asked.

"Stevie . . . ," Carole began, and stopped.

"What?" Stevie said, sounding annoyed. "Look, Lisa, I know it's hard for you to talk to your mom, but this isn't just a haircut. This is boarding school! You can't just let your parents send you to Horror High with a bunch of Veronica types."

To her surprise, Lisa felt a flash of anger. All of a sudden she wasn't so thrilled to hear Stevie mocking Wentworth.

Stevie was ranting, "To think that someone like you could go to that no-good, worthless—"

"Okay, Stevie, I get the point," Lisa broke in. "But

the fact is I'm going there. Maybe it won't be so bad, all right?"

*Not so bad?* Stevie thought. *Is Lisa out of her mind?* "I just meant—"

"Look, I know what you meant. I have to go now, anyway. I have to finish my homework," Lisa said coldly.

Searching for something she could say to cheer Lisa up, Carole asked, "Will you be at Pine Hollow tomorrow?"

"Yeah, I guess so," Lisa said. With hardly a good-bye, she hung up.

Carole and Stevie stayed on the line to talk, but neither of them had much to say. It was the most shocking news they'd ever had. They had to absorb it before they could make any sense of it. "See you tomorrow?" Carole asked quietly.

"Yeah, see you then," Stevie said. After she put the receiver down, she sat at her desk, staring into space. Lisa was going to boarding school. It didn't seem possible, but it was. Mrs. Atwood was finally going to have Lisa where she wanted her: climbing the social ladder. Stevie couldn't believe how dumb she'd been not to think of the possibility of Lisa's getting a scholarship. There were a number of students at Fenton Hall on scholarship. And naturally, Lisa was a prime candidate. But realizing her own mistake hadn't been the most dis-

77

turbing part of the conversation for Stevie. What troubled her most was the way Lisa had seemed to change her mind about Wentworth. A part of Stevie realized that she had hurt Lisa's feelings by insulting the school, but a part of her just didn't care. Shouldn't Lisa know the truth about the school? That she was way too good for it? That going there would be the biggest mistake of her life?

LISA WENT THROUGH the next day of school in a daze. She couldn't concentrate on any of her subjects. In third-period math, her teacher called on her to demonstrate a simple problem for the class. Lisa couldn't do it. She stood at the blackboard with a piece of chalk in her hand, unable to remember how to begin. Finally she looked up at Mr. Ramirez, her eyes bright with tears. "I don't know how to do it," she said in a choked voice.

Mr. Ramirez looked at her with concern. "Have you been getting enough sleep, Lisa?" he asked quietly. "You look tired."

"That must be it," Lisa said. She didn't want to tell

Mr. Ramirez why a math problem was making her so upset. Besides, it was true that she had hardly slept at all the night before. Even though she'd followed her mother's advice to go to bed early, she had tossed and turned for hours.

"Do you want to go lie down somewhere?" Mr. Ramirez asked.

Lisa shook her head. "No, that's okay. I'll be fine."

"All right, then. Go ahead and take your seat. Class is almost over anyway," Mr. Ramirez said. "Now," he continued in a louder voice, "who wants to tell me how to multiply two unknowns when . . ."

Lisa slunk back to her seat, feeling the class's curious eyes on her. She knew they were wondering why she hadn't been able to do the problem. After class, a few people asked her if she was okay. Lisa nodded. She couldn't bring herself to tell them anything. At breakfast her mother had reminded her to give her teachers the news right away. That way they could begin processing her transfer forms. But after English and French and now math, Lisa still hadn't said a word to anyone. She knew that if she started to talk, she would start to cry.

Lisa was so caught up in her own troubled thoughts that she almost didn't see Carole coming down the hall toward her.

"Lisa! Lisa, hey!" Carole called, hurrying over, her

face a mask of worry. The girls often ran into one another at school, even though Lisa was in the grade above Carole.

Lisa looked up, glad to see the only person at school who knew her secret. "Hi, Carole," she said.

"Hi," Carole said. Then she asked timidly, "So, nothing has changed since last night?"

Lisa looked down at her books. "Nope. I'm still going to Wentworth."

"And you can't say anything to your mother about how you really feel?" Carole asked. She knew she was taking a chance of upsetting Lisa even more. But in her heart of hearts, she believed that Stevie was right—that Lisa's only chance was to say something, even if it meant letting her mother down.

Lisa shook her head. "You should see how excited she is, Carole. This morning, as I was getting ready for school, some woman from the Garden Club called. She told my mother she had heard that I was applying to Wentworth. Her daughter goes there, and she wanted to know if I'd been accepted and what my plans were."

"That's so rude!" Carole said, disgusted that anyone would stoop so low as to actually call the Atwoods to see if Lisa had gotten into Wentworth.

"I know. But naturally my mother was thrilled to get the call. She went on and on about how much I loved

81

the school. She even told the woman about my scholar-ship," Lisa said.

"It is a big honor," Carole said.

Before Lisa could reply, the bell for the next class rang. It was Lisa's lunch period, but Carole had social studies and had to run. "Look, I'll see you at the barn, okay?" Carole said. She felt bad that she couldn't skip her class and stay with Lisa.

"Sure—and don't worry, Carole. I'll be fine," Lisa said, trying to sound brave. She headed to the cafeteria, got her lunch, and sat down by herself, praying that nobody would join her. She couldn't bear the thought of having to make conversation with anyone. It was strange to think that in a couple of weeks, she would be eating in the Wentworth cafeteria. Who would she talk to then? Would any of the girls become her friends? Maybe there were other scholarship students and they would all eat lunch together. Then again, maybe she was the only one. Her mother had told her about all the social opportunities at Wentworth. But what kind of op-portunities would there be if Lisa never made friends?

For the tenth time that day, Lisa felt like crying. She felt a tear well up in her eye and start to trickle down her cheek. But as soon as she began to cry, she stopped herself. She had to quit feeling sorry for herself, just to get through the day. Moping about Wentworth wasn't going to do her any good. Maybe she could try looking on the bright side. Maybe Carole and her mother were right. It *was* a big honor to go to such a prestigious school on a full scholarship. She should be grateful for all her mother had done to get her in.

It was no surprise that Stevie couldn't understand. It was easy for her to put Wentworth down. Her parents had plenty of money. But Lisa's mother wanted her daughter to have more than she'd had. She thought Wentworth would set Lisa on the road to success.

The more Lisa thought about what Stevie had said, the angrier she got. Maybe Stevie was just jealous. Everybody knew that Wentworth had one of the nicest riding facilities in Virginia. Maybe it would be fun to go there. Maybe Stevie had wanted to go there and her parents had said no. A little voice inside Lisa told her she wasn't being honest with herself, but she ignored it. She hadn't let herself get angry at anyone for a long time. And in a way, getting mad felt better than letting herself be miserable.

TUESDAY AFTERNOONS The Saddle Club and a few other students, including Veronica, had a riding lesson with Max. Stevie, Lisa, and Carole liked to get their horses ready a little early so that they could talk while they warmed up together. Once the lesson started, Max was a

83

stickler for no talking. But this Tuesday, the three of them found themselves lingering instead of hurrying while they groomed Belle, Prancer, and Starlight. The truth was, none of them wanted to talk because none of them knew what to say. There was still tension between Lisa and Stevie from the night before. And Carole wasn't sure if she should mention it or pretend it didn't exist. When it came to people, Carole could never figure them out. Horses were so much easier to understand.

When the three of them went to the tack room to get their saddles and bridles, the silence was awkward.

"Hey, did you hear that Veronica volunteered to clean my tack yesterday?" Stevie asked, trying to make conversation.

Carole chuckled, relieved at the safe topic. "You've got to put a stop to it, Stevie, unless you're really considering her for the job."

"Oh, I will—just as soon as she finishes the tack. She still has to do the bridle," Stevie said with a laugh. She stole a glance at Lisa to see if she would smile, but Lisa's face was grim. Stevie and Carole exchanged worried glances. They knew Lisa was upset. What they didn't know was how to get her to talk to them.

Stevie decided to try the direct route. "Lisa?" she said. "I'm sorry for what I said about Wentworth. I thought you thought the same thing, or else I wouldn't have—"

"Well, for a change, maybe you should think about what you say *before* you say it," Lisa snapped, her face turning red.

"But you said you didn't like it, either," Stevie said in a small voice that didn't sound anything like her own.

"Maybe you should have realized that my feelings have changed now that I'm going to go to school there," Lisa retorted.

"But—but—do you really want to go there?" Stevie said in a rush. She knew she was pushing it by asking that question yet again, but she just had to. She couldn't sit back and pretend that if Lisa went to Wentworth, everything would be all right.

Lisa looked from Stevie to Carole, her face threatening to crumple. She was about to reply when the door swung open and Veronica walked in.

"Lisa!" Veronica said in a gushy voice. "I heard the great news. So you're going to be a Wentworth girl. Congratulations!"

"Thanks," Lisa muttered.

"Listen," Veronica went on, oblivious to the tense atmosphere she'd walked in on, "I was thinking it would be fun for you and my friend Ashley Briggs to get to know one another. She's coming to visit me next weekend, so I'll ask my mother if I can have you over for dinner."

Stevie looked scornfully at Veronica. It made her sick to see Veronica acting nice toward Lisa just because of Wentworth. "Why are you so friendly all of a sudden?" she demanded. "Is it because Lisa's going to a snobby boarding school—"

"Why should you care?" Veronica snapped.

"Because I care about my friends," Stevie retorted. "Unlike you, Veronica, I don't choose my friends based on what school they go to. So don't bother trying to be all nice to Lisa. Because she can see right through your little—"

"Stevie!" Lisa cried. "Would you mind staying out of it?"

Stevie turned. She stared at Lisa, mouth open, for several seconds. Without another word she grabbed her saddle, bridle, and hard hat and stormed out of the tack room.

"Boy, with friends like that, who needs enemies?" Veronica said. "Now, Lisa—"

"Just leave me alone! Leave me alone!" Lisa wailed. She fled the room as fast as Stevie had.

"Well, excu-u-use me," Veronica said.

A few seconds later Stevie poked her head back in. "By the way, Veronica, I wouldn't make you cochair of the dance committee if my life depended on it," she said.

"Good!" Veronica spat back. "Because I wouldn't take it if *my* life depended on it!"

The door slammed for the third time. Carole glowered at Veronica but said nothing. It was all too much to comprehend—better to concentrate on horses for an hour and figure out the human mess later. The lesson started in five minutes; at this point, they were going to be late. And any second now, Max was going to come in and give them a harsh lecture for making so much noise in the barn. It was a miracle that he hadn't already.

TRYING TO CHOKE back her tears, Lisa managed to get Prancer tacked up. Her fingers fumbled with the billet straps on the girth, then with the bit, but finally Prancer was ready. Lisa led her out and got on. Once she was mounted, however, she couldn't face going to the lesson. She didn't even care about the questions Max would ask when she failed to show up. She knew it would be no use trying to learn anything.

Hardly thinking, she spurred Prancer toward the trail. She trotted and cantered until they were a good distance from Pine Hollow. Then she slowed Prancer to a walk and gave her a long rein. Slouched in the saddle, she let the mare loaf along, not even stopping her from grabbing bites of grass and leaves. And finally, out on the trail where no one could hear her, Lisa let herself cry. She cried and cried, thinking back over the past twenty-four hours. Prancer turned her head around and nudged Lisa's stirrup to ask what was wrong. That only made Lisa cry harder, realizing that she wouldn't be able to take Prancer with her to Wentworth. Prancer wasn't hers, and anyway her parents would never be able to afford the board. It probably cost half of their salaries.

"I wonder who will ride you when I'm gone," Lisa said, stroking Prancer's chestnut neck. "If only they had scholarships for horses, too. Then you could come with me and it wouldn't be so bad. I could tell you about the other girls, and you could tell me about the other horses. . . ."

Lisa prolonged the ride, letting Prancer wander from meadow to meadow. Not until it started to get dark did she turn back toward the stable. She wondered how many more rides she would have before she left. Maybe it would be better not to come anymore. Dragging out the good-bye would only make things harder. Sure, she could come back and visit, but it would never be the same. In fact, it already felt different. With the way things were between her and Stevie, it felt as if The Saddle Club had broken up. And that was by far the blackest part of it all.

THE PARENTS OF The Saddle Club almost never allowed sleepovers on school nights. They agreed that the girls saw plenty of one another at Pine Hollow, on the weekends, and during the trips they often took together. So Sunday through Thursday nights the three of them were expected to stay in, do their homework, and go to bed at a reasonable time. But every once in a while, a circumstance arose that was dire enough for the girls to convince their parents that they absolutely had to have a weeknight sleepover. When Lisa disappeared on Prancer instead of coming to the lesson, Stevie and Carole agreed that this was one of those nights. They simply had to have a two-thirds meeting of The Saddle Club. Right away. No matter what it took. So after two anxious phone calls and some hasty arrangements between Colonel Hanson and Mr. and Mrs. Lake, Carole found herself at the Lakes' for the evening.

She and Stevie wasted no time. They went directly up to Stevie's room to put their heads together and find a way of saving Lisa from Wentworth Manor. They felt a little guilty about having a meeting without Lisa, but, as Stevie put it, "You can't save a drowning man by jumping into the ocean."

"Huh?" Carole said.

"Never mind—it's just an expression," Stevie replied.

Mrs. Lake rapped on the door and poked her head in. "I thought this was an emergency meeting of The Saddle Club," she said, putting down a plate of cookies for them. "The *whole* Saddle Club."

Stevie and Carole looked at one another, not knowing if they should explain Lisa's absence. "It is, Mom, but you see, Lisa *is* the emergency," Stevie said.

"She's not sick, is she?" Mrs. Lake asked quickly.

"No," Stevie said. Somehow she wasn't sure her mother would be very sympathetic when she found out what they were meeting about. She had purposely left that vague when she'd asked permission to invite Carole over, emphasizing that it was definitely an emergency and that her mother should trust her judgment. "She's not sick."

"Then where is she?" Mrs. Lake asked bluntly. "What's the emergency?"

"We have to save her from being sent to Wentworth Manor," Stevie said just as bluntly.

"Lisa's going to boarding school?" Mrs. Lake asked.

"Next week," Carole said.

Mrs. Lake frowned. "So, I still don't see what the emergency is. If Lisa and her parents have decided that that's the best place for her, why should you interfere?"

"But Mom!" Stevie protested. "*Lisa* didn't decide anything! She just went along with it because her mom wants her to go there. She'd hate it there! And she'd miss us and The Saddle Club and Pine Hollow!"

"I'm sure it's hard for you to imagine her going away, but make sure you're thinking about Lisa, sweetheart. It's her future. Wentworth might be a great opportunity for her," Mrs. Lake said.

Stevie waited until her mother had left to respond. "That is so typical!" she hissed. "Parents always band together! I've *heard* my mother call Wentworth a chi-chi riding school, but now she's siding with Mrs. Atwood."

"To be fair, maybe we should consider the possibility

that Lisa would be better off at Wentworth," Carole said reluctantly. She and Stevie were silent for about five seconds.

"She wouldn't," Stevie and Carole said at the same time.

"If she wanted to go there, she would still be sad to leave, but the point is, she's not acting sad," Stevie reasoned. "She's way beyond sad."

"She's miserable," Carole agreed. "And confused and upset and tortured. And this is one time when we know how she feels and her parents don't. If they knew how much she hated Wentworth, they would never want her to go there."

"Well . . . ," Stevie said doubtfully, remembering Mrs. Atwood's history of pressuring Lisa into things.

"No, seriously, Stevie. Her mother might make her look at the place, but she wouldn't make her *go* there," Carole insisted.

"I guess you're right," Stevie conceded. Frustrated, she crossed her arms over her chest and sat back on her bed. "If only we could get Lisa to talk to her mother!"

"But she won't—or can't," Carole said, sighing.

"And you know what really gets me?" Stevie said, after thinking for a few minutes. "Everyone keeps mentioning the great opportunities at Wentworth, but how great are they? I think the greatest opportunity is for Lisa to stay right where she is, where she's always been happy."

"And successful," Carole added. "She aces everything, but she has enough competition so she doesn't get bored." Carole knew about the crowd of supersmart kids Lisa competed with academically. She'd often heard Lisa say that certain of her classmates, as well as her teachers, kept her on her toes.

"That's one thing she won't have at Wentworth," Stevie said scornfully. "None of those girls could be half as smart as Lisa. All they care about is their appearance."

"Do you think Mrs. Atwood realizes that it's not that great academically?" Carole asked.

Stevie shrugged. "Who knows? She's probably so caught up in how prestigious it is that she's forgotten all about academics."

The girls talked for almost an hour without thinking up any solutions. They wanted to call Lisa and beg her to talk to her parents, but they were scared that that would backfire. They were afraid that Lisa, sick of their interfering, would refuse to talk to them, upset that they were persisting in making it worse for her.

When Mrs. Lake knocked on the door again to tell them to go to bed, they were beginning to feel desperate.

"You'll have to get your own breakfast in the morning, girls," Mrs. Lake told them, "because I'm not going to be here. I'm leaving very early to get my hair cut before work."

"Where are you getting it cut?" Stevie asked idly. She could never keep straight which salon her mother went to because she always seemed to be changing hairdressers.

"I'm going back to Cosmo Cuts," said Mrs. Lake. "Everyone agrees it's the best. It's owned by that man—"

"Charles," Stevie and Carole said in unison.

Mrs. Lake looked at them, surprised. "How did you know?"

"Mrs. Atwood took Lisa there, and Mrs. diAngelo and Veronica get their hair done there once a week," Carole explained.

"It sounds like the place to go, then," Mrs. Lake said. "There's cereal and fruit for the morning, okay?"

At her mother's insistence, Stevie turned the lights out. She waited until she heard her mother go into her own bedroom and shut the door. Then she turned the lights back on—and sat bolt upright. "Carole," she said, trying to keep her voice steady, "do you think that if Lisa's mother suddenly changed her mind

94

about Wentworth, Lisa would feel okay about not going?"

Carole stared at her friend curiously. "I think that if Lisa could get out of this without having to upset her mother, she would do it in a second. Why? What do you have in mind?"

"Remember what you told me Lisa said about the hair salon?" Stevie asked.

Carole considered Stevie's question for a moment. "You mean what the women were saying about Max and Veronica?"

"Not what they were saying, but *that* they were saying it," Stevie said breathlessly. "Lisa said that Cosmo Cuts was a great place to eavesdrop—a great place to overhear things."

"So?" Carole said. As usual, she was utterly failing to follow Stevie's train of thought.

"Well, what if Mrs. Atwood were to overhear negative things about Wentworth at her next appointment?" Stevie said. She paused to let her idea sink in, watching Carole process the suggestion. "What if someone were to say that Wentworth is a horrible school?"

"Then Mrs. Atwood might decide that it's not such a great opportunity for Lisa after all," Carole said slowly. "But she couldn't hear it from just anyone."

"No, she'd have to hear it from a socially prominent person," Stevie said, thinking hard.

"Who? Your mother? I doubt she'd want to take part in a setup like that," Carole said.

The very thought of her mother's agreeing to be in cahoots with them made Stevie laugh. "She sure wouldn't, and she'd give us a lecture on scheming behind people's backs, too."

"So what are you getting at?" Carole asked. Stevie's idea was all well and good, but the chances of some person's bad-mouthing Wentworth while Mrs. Atwood was there were almost nil. Obviously they had to get someone to do it. But adults were annoying that way. They'd want to know all about the plan, and then they'd probably try to put a stop to it instead of joining forces.

"I'm not sure exactly," Stevie admitted. "But if we could think of someone . . ."

"Wait a minute," Carole said. *"Wait a minute!* It's perfect—oh my gosh, it's perfect!"

"What? Who?" Stevie demanded.

"Who gets her hair done there every week?" Carole asked.

Stevie's eyes grew large. "And hates Wentworth already!"

"Mrs. diAngelo!" they both cried—or at least, they

would have cried, except that they were whispering so that they wouldn't get into trouble with Stevie's mother.

"Do you think if somebody prompted her, she would say bad things about Wentworth?" Carole asked.

"I know she would. I've heard her rant and rave about the place. The question is, who's going to do the prompting?" Stevie said.

"We certainly can't—that would be way too obvious," Carole said. One by one, she considered people and rejected them.

"Oh no!" Stevie moaned all of a sudden.

"What?" Carole said. "What is it?" She could tell that Stevie was about four moves ahead of her. She had seen through to the end of the plan.

Stevie let out a long-suffering sigh. "I just realized who I'm going to have to pick to be cochair of the dance committee."

Carole's face lit up. "Veronica!" she exclaimed. She didn't need Stevie to explain any further. She understood perfectly: Stevie was going to bribe Veronica with the dance committee job. Veronica would already be at the salon with her mother. It would be easy for her to casually mention Wentworth Manor. If all went as planned, Mrs. diAngelo would do the rest. "Brilliant," Carole breathed. "Absolutely brilliant."

"There's a flaw, though," Stevie said. "I just realized what it is. We're going to have to involve Lisa. We can't wait until Mrs. Atwood needs another appointment. That could be weeks, and chances are it would be on the wrong day of the week. Lisa is going to have to get her mother to go to Cosmo Cuts at the same day and time as Veronica's mother."

"You're right," Carole agreed. After reflecting for a minute, she said, "But you know, I don't think that's a flaw. I think we should talk to Lisa and tell her about this. It's her life, after all. I say we have emergency meeting number two tomorrow after school at TD's, only this time with the whole Saddle Club. I'll speak to Lisa in school. I'm sure I can get her to come if I pretend it's for one last time before she leaves."

The two girls went over the plan again in detail. Both of them would have felt better if Lisa had been there with her notebook to jot it all down and look for loopholes. But they had to do the best they could without her. When they met tomorrow, they had to present her with a finished plan.

"I can't believe we're putting Lisa's fate into the di-Angelos' hands," Carole said, finally putting her head on her pillow.

Without answering, Stevie got out of bed and began

98

to rummage through the wastebasket under her desk. "What are you doing?" Carole asked curiously.

"I'm hunting for that list of possible themes for the dance that Veronica gave me. It looks like we might have to have a 'Princess of Fenton Hall' dance after all—with you-know-who wearing the crown of honor!"

STEVIE HAD SWALLOWED her pride many times before. She had begged for mercy and groveled for forgiveness. But the thought of groveling in front of Veronica made her feel physically ill. She was determined to keep the ball in her court. If she let on that Veronica was the key to their entire plan, Veronica would lord it over her no end. The next morning at school, Stevie planned her attack. She decided to catch Veronica on her way to lunch. She hoped Veronica would be hungry so that her defenses would be down.

First Stevie stalked her prey. The hall was bustling with students, but Veronica stood out in her brand-new sweater and skirt, with her elaborately coiffed black hair. Sometimes Stevie wondered if she ever wore the same thing twice or just threw her clothes out after a day at school. Once Stevie located her, she doubled back down the hall as fast as she could so that she could run into Veronica—literally. "Oh, excuse me!" Stevie said, looking up at the last minute.

"Very funny," Veronica said sarcastically.

"I didn't mean to bump into you," Stevie protested, "honestly."

"Sure, Stevie," Veronica said. "I'll believe that the day you make me head of the dance committee."

Stevie couldn't believe the opening Veronica had given her. It was too good to be true. "Then I guess you'll have to believe me, because I decided last night, and you're my cochair."

Instead of jumping for joy, Veronica looked suspiciously at Stevie. Stevie knew that now was her moment to shine. If she acted strange about it, Veronica would guess she was up to something. "Yup. I thought about it," Stevie said nonchalantly, "and I figured you're the right person for the job."

Veronica narrowed her eyes. She looked unconvinced.

"Even after yesterday? Stevie, if this is some kind of a joke—"

"It's not a joke. Look, we both know we're not best friends, right?"

"That's for sure," Veronica said with a short laugh.

"Well, that's the whole point," Stevie said.

"What is?" Veronica asked.

"I want this dance to be great. And in order for it to be great, a lot of people have to come. So it would be stupid for me to pick one of my friends to be cochair. A friend would only bring in the same crowd that I would. But if I pick you, you'll bring in a whole other crowd of people." To herself, Stevie added, *A whole crowd of snobs and jerks*.

Veronica was many things, but she wasn't stupid. Stevie watched her face and could see that she understood the logic behind Stevie's plan. Stevie was rather impressed with the plan herself. Miss Fenton would have to be convinced that the two of them could work together without killing each other, but Stevie wasn't worried about that—she'd been sweet-talking her elders for as long as she could remember, with great results.

"All right. I guess I'll do it," Veronica said. "If you need me that badly."

Stevie could tell that Veronica was trying to hide her

102

excitement. After swearing at Pine Hollow that she wouldn't take the job, she wouldn't want to let on how happy she was to get it now.

"There's just one little thing you have to do," Stevie said, moving in for the kill.

"I think I've already done quite enough," Veronica said, bristling.

"Oh, don't worry. This is easy. When are your and your mother's next appointments at Cosmo Cuts?" Stevie asked.

Veronica sneered. "What, you want my mother to treat you to a cut there? Your hair could sure use some help, but couldn't you ask your own mother?"

"Just tell me when you're going," Stevie said, her patience ebbing fast.

"What's today? Wednesday? So it's tomorrow—my mother goes Thursdays at four, and I go at four-thirty. We have to stagger our appointments because we'll both only go to Charles. He's the best, you know. He . . ."

Stevie reeled for a minute at the news that they only had a day to organize everything. But recovering herself, she took Veronica by the arm and led her down the hall. When Veronica had finished going on about Charles, Stevie said, as casually as possible, "Here's what you have to do. . . ."

\* \* \*

CAROLE WAITED ANXIOUSLY at TD's, the local ice cream parlor. She was sitting alone in The Saddle Club's usual booth. It was just four o'clock. She knew Stevie would get there any minute, but she was worried about Lisa. Lisa had been reluctant to meet them. She'd told Carole that she didn't want to get into another argument with Stevie about Wentworth. And even though she'd finally agreed to come, Carole couldn't relax until she'd walked in the door.

At five after, Lisa arrived, followed by Stevie. Carole breathed a sigh of relief. Once they were all seated, Carole and Stevie looked at one another. Stevie nodded almost imperceptibly.

"Lisa," Carole began, "we got you here under false pretenses."

Lisa frowned but stayed silent, letting Carole continue.

Carole spoke quietly but urgently, turning so that she could look right at Lisa. "We got you here to tell you that we have a plan. We think we know a way to save you from going to Wentworth without upsetting your mother. But what we have to know is the bottom line: Do you want to be saved?"

Lisa swallowed hard. "Yes," she said in a dry voice.

"Yippee!" Stevie shouted at the top of her lungs.

104

One of the waitresses walked lazily over to them. "I take it you want to order," she asked, totally unfazed by Stevie's outburst.

"Actually, we still need about five minutes," Stevie said meekly.

"Sure, kids, whatever," the waitress said, retreating to the counter.

"So, you don't want to go there?" Carole asked.

Lisa shifted uncomfortably in her seat. She looked at Stevie, then looked down. "I feel silly admitting it now, after I made such a fuss, but no, I don't want to go to Wentworth." At Stevie and Carole's expectant looks, she went on, "I dread going there. I'd hate it—I know I would. I'd miss my parents and you guys and Prancer and Max and Mrs. Reg and my teachers more than I can imagine. Heck, I'd even miss the obnoxious boys who take over the student lounge. But I told my mother the school was nice because she made such a big effort to get me accepted there, with a scholarship." By this time Lisa was half laughing, half sobbing—it was such a relief to talk to Carole and Stevie again.

Carole put an arm around Lisa. Stevie muttered something about being sorry for interfering. Lisa refused to accept the apology. "I'm the one who should be sorry," she said.

With the air cleared, Stevie got down to the plan.

Listening intently, Lisa interrupted to ask a question. "How do I get my mother to go there tomorrow, though?"

"Tell her you want her to look especially nice now that she's going to be a Wentworth mom, so you're treating her to a shampoo and set," Stevie said.

"A shampoo and set won't last a whole week, though," Lisa pointed out.

Stevie smiled. Normally she hated to find problems with her schemes, but it was so great to have Lisa back on the scene that she didn't mind. "Okay, how about a manicure, then?"

Lisa shook her head. "She does her own nails."

"I've got it," Carole said. "A facial."

"Great idea," Stevie said. "Facials are really special, aren't they? I know my mom only gets them, like, once a year."

Lisa grinned. "Yeah, they're so special they cost around sixty dollars."

Stevie winced. "Ouch."

"But if we all chip in, that's only twenty apiece," Carole said. "Agreed?"

"Agreed," Stevie said. Then she added sheepishly, "As long as I can borrow twenty dollars."

Lisa and Carole laughed. They were both savers, but

they knew that money burned a hole in Stevie's pocket. "Are you sure it's not too much?" Lisa asked.

"Of course we're sure. Think of what we'll save in stamps and long-distance phone calls," Carole said.

"Okay, so a facial it is. But what if I can't get an appointment for four o'clock? That salon is so popular, you usually have to wait weeks," said Lisa.

Stevie's hazel eyes twinkled. "We'll solve that right now," she said. She got up and went to the pay phone in the corner of the ice cream parlor.

"What do you think she's doing?" Lisa asked.

"Turning on the Stevie Lake charm," Carole guessed.

A few minutes later Stevie rejoined them at the table. "Boy, they're tough at Cosmo Cuts. But I got the appointment. At quarter past four tomorrow, which, by the way, is your mother's birthday," Stevie told Lisa.

"It is?" Lisa asked. "You told them it was my mother's birthday?"

"Yes, and you forgot to make the appointment and you felt terrible because you saved up your money for weeks to get her this facial and you'd never forgive yourself if she couldn't go tomorrow. Just a little white lie."

"That's all it took?" Carole asked.

"That and some fake crying," Stevie said with a grin.

"Nice work," Carole said. "It's too bad we won't be there to watch the scene take place."

"Not be there? What do you mean?" Stevie asked.

"We can't be there, Stevie! It would be way too obvious that something strange was going on if you and I just happened to be hanging out at the salon tomorrow," Carole said.

"You're right," Stevie said glumly. "The best part of my plan was going to be watching it put into action. I guess we'll have to hear what happens from Lisa."

"You kids ready to order yet?" the waitress asked, reappearing in front of them.

"We sure are," Stevie replied, perking up. "Girls?"

"I'll have a small chocolate cone with chocolate sprinkles," Lisa said.

"And I'll have a dish of mint chip," Carole said.

"And I'll have the peanut butter special," said Stevie.

"We don't have a peanut butter special," the waitress said flatly.

"I know: I'm making it up," Stevie replied. "Let's see . . . one scoop each of strawberry and fudge ripple ice cream with marshmallow and pineapple topping, chocolate sprinkles, and a cherry."

"There's no peanut butter in there," the waitress said.

Stevie smiled patronizingly. "Of course not," she said. "That's why it's special."

11

"YOU REALLY SHOULDN'T have spent your money, dear," Mrs. Atwood said as she and Lisa sat down in the waiting area at Cosmo Cuts.

"I wanted to, Mom," Lisa said, looking around anxiously. She had been a complete wreck all day, worrying about the plan. First her mother had refused the gift, saying it was too much for Lisa to spend. Then, once Lisa had talked her into it, she had thought it was strange that Lisa wanted to come. So Lisa had made up some excuse about how nice the salon was—how she would enjoy going there just to hang out for a while. Carole and Stevie had agreed that since they couldn't be present, Lisa had to be. Somebody had to make sure Veronica played her part.

Now that they were there, Lisa could hardly believe that she'd gotten her mother over to the salon on time. Thankfully, Veronica and her mother were already there. Veronica was getting her nails done while her mother sat in Charles's chair in the middle of the room. Lisa put up a hand and waved at Veronica. In response Veronica gave the barest nod in her direction.

Lisa sat down and began to flip through a magazine. She couldn't concentrate on the articles or even the pictures. The weirdest part of the plan was that she and Veronica were sort of on the same side. Stevie had assured her that Veronica wouldn't mess up, but Lisa was worried all the same. What if Veronica never said anything? Or what if Lisa's mother failed to hear for some reason? Or if Mrs. diAngelo didn't take the bait? What if she had changed her mind about Wentworth and said she loved the place?

"Isn't that Barb diAngelo?" Mrs. Atwood whispered.

"What, Mom?" Lisa said with a start.

"I said, isn't that Veronica diAngelo's mother? Barbara, I think her name is."

"It sure is," Lisa said enthusiastically.

"We've met at Pine Hollow a number of times," Mrs. Atwood said.

"Oh, really?" Lisa said, thrilled that her mother had noticed Mrs. diAngelo already.

"Yes, dear. I've told you before you should always be very polite to her and her daughter. The diAngelos are very important people in Willow Creek, you know—and far beyond Willow Creek, too. You should keep that in mind."

"I will, Mom," Lisa promised.

Just then Mrs. diAngelo let out a loud cackle. "Charles, you are too funny!" she said.

"Do you have to laugh so loudly, Mother?" Veronica whined from her position at the manicure table, a few chairs away.

Mrs. diAngelo glared at her daughter via the mirror. "Mind your manners, Veronica!" she snapped.

"But, Mother, it's embarrassing!" Veronica said, pouting.

Lisa noticed that the other women in the salon had stopped talking and were listening to the diAngelos argue. Despite Charles's protests, Mrs. diAngelo swiveled her head around to speak to Veronica. "That's enough, young lady!" she barked. "Or you're going home."

Lisa felt her blood run cold at the words *going home*. Veronica *couldn't* go home. If she got sent home, Lisa would get sent to Wentworth Manor. Period. This was her only chance.

**111**

"I'd rather go home than be in a public place with you embarrassing me," Veronica said, loudly enough for her mother to hear.

Mrs. diAngelo jumped up from Charles's chair, smock and all, and marched over to her daughter. "That's it. I won't take any more of this from you. Go wait in the car. Do you hear me?"

"But my nails aren't even dry!" Veronica wailed.

Lisa held her breath, not daring to move.

"Mrs. diAngelo, please!" Charles said, waving his scissors and comb in annoyance. "You're ruining your cut! I won't have this in my salon! Sit down this instant or I won't finish your hair!"

Mrs. diAngelo glanced at herself in the mirror. Her expression changed from anger to horror when she saw how bad her half-done hair looked. One side looked normal, but the other side was clipped up, going in all directions. Without another word to Veronica, she sat back down in Charles's chair, apologizing profusely for interfering with his "art."

Lisa almost fell out of her own chair with relief. She'd barely had time to recover when a woman came to take her mother over to the "skin-care corner," where they gave facials.

"Happy Birthday, Mrs. Atwood," the woman said cheerily.

Lisa froze for the second time. Her mother gave the woman an odd look. On her way over to the corner, Mrs. Atwood turned around to look at Lisa. She made a funny face, pointed at the woman, and mouthed, "Crazy." Lisa felt her heart start beating again. Obviously, her mother had no idea why the woman thought it was her birthday. But Lisa felt as if *she* was the one going crazy. If Veronica didn't get to the point soon, she would probably run screaming out of Cosmo Cuts, never to return. The situation was nerve-racking beyond belief, especially without Carole and Stevie there to reassure her.

The minutes ticked by, and still Veronica said nothing. Mrs. Atwood had a clay mask put on her face. Veronica and her mother switched places, Veronica to get her hair done and Mrs. diAngelo to get a manicure. The facial woman wiped the mask off Mrs. Atwood's face. Charles began to snip away at Veronica's hair. The manicurist finished Mrs. diAngelo's left hand and started on her right. And still Veronica said nothing! The anticipation was more than Lisa could bear. Suddenly she realized that Veronica was probably delaying the conversation on purpose—to torture Lisa. Enraged, Lisa jumped up and walked over to Charles's chair.

"Hi, Veronica," she said loudly. "I saw you getting your hair done, and I wanted to say hello."

113

"That's nice," Veronica said flatly.

"Don't turn your head like that," Charles ordered. He pumped up the chair several times to raise Veronica. "This is a very difficult cut."

"Yes, Charles," Veronica said meekly. Then she added pointedly, "It's just so distracting to have someone talking to me."

"I was just leaving, anyway," Lisa said. "I didn't come over here to *start a conversation*," she added. With a final glare at Veronica, she turned and walked back to the couch, listening intently as she sat down.

"A friend of yours?" Charles asked.

"Not really," Veronica said, not bothering to lower her voice.

"Beautiful hair," Charles said.

"Thanks, Charles."

"I was talking about her," Charles said, gesturing toward Lisa with his comb.

Lisa smiled to herself. Evidently Charles was such a popular hairstylist that he could get away with saying anything he wanted to his customers. She knew Veronica wouldn't dare object. If she did, Charles might refuse to cut her hair.

"How are you doing, dear?"

Lisa looked up at the sound of her mother's voice. Mrs. Atwood was now getting a facial massage. "I'm fine,

Mom. I was just thinking about *school*," Lisa said, emphasizing the last word for Veronica's benefit.

Veronica gave Lisa a sour look, as best she could without turning her head. But she seemed to sense that she couldn't put off her job any longer. "Aren't you going to Wentworth Manor in a couple of weeks, Lisa?" she asked.

"Ye-es," Lisa said cautiously. She hadn't expected to be made part of the conversation.

"Mummy, did you hear that?" Veronica said. "Lisa is going to Wentworth Manor."

Her heart thumping, Lisa stole a glance at her mother. Mrs. Atwood was staring at Mrs. diAngelo, waiting to see what her response would be.

Mrs. diAngelo's eyes grew large. She drew in a breath. Her mouth curled back in utter distaste. "Wentworth Manor?" she repeated, her voice shaking with intensity. "Did you say Wentworth Manor?"

"Yes," Veronica said.

The whole salon grew quiet. The stylists stopped styling, the manicurist stopped manicuring. The employees, the customers, even Charles turned and stared at Mrs. diAngelo, the most important woman in Willow Creek. Mrs. diAngelo exploded.

"I thought I told you never to mention that school to me!" she cried. "How dare you! That horrible school!

115

Nobody in their right mind would send their daughter there! It's a school for misfits, outcasts from society, rejects! I'd rather send a girl to jail than send her to Wentworth Manor. Jail would do more for her social standing. It's a pigsty of a school—a rat's nest, do you hear me?"

There was a long pause. Finally Charles spoke up. "I never much liked those Wentworth girls, either," he said, cutting away at Veronica's hair.

Seemingly unaware that she had just made a huge scene, Mrs. diAngelo sniffed a few times. "All right, continue," she said to the manicurist.

Lisa was speechless. Mrs. diAngelo had carried on beyond her wildest dreams. Lisa's mother looked extremely upset. Lisa knew she was mulling over Mrs. diAngelo's words. Hearing the most important woman in Willow Creek describe Wentworth as a school for rejects would completely ruin her idea of Wentworth as *the* school to send her daughter to.

Sure enough, as soon as her facial was done, Lisa's mother threw on her coat on and hurried over. "Come on, dear, let's get going," she urged. Lisa knew that her mother wanted to beat the diAngelos out so that she wouldn't have to speak to them.

In the car driving home, Mrs. Atwood cleared her throat a couple of times. Finally she said to Lisa, "You know, dear, I've been thinking. Maybe we acted too fast

116

getting you into Wentworth for this semester. Maybe you ought to think about it for January or next September. I want to make a few calls when we get home. . . ."

The plan had worked perfectly, but for some reason, Lisa wasn't happy. Instead of wanting to rush home and tell Stevie and Carole the good news, she felt deflated.

When they got home, Lisa went up to her room. She lay on her bed. She stared at the phone. She knew Stevie and Carole would be dying to know how the plan had gone. She knew she should share the good news— that her mother had fallen for it. But as she contemplated calling them, she began to realize something: The plan had worked, but the plan itself was all wrong. Nobody, but nobody, should have to *trick* her mother about something so important.

It wasn't Carole and Stevie's fault—they'd only been acting in Lisa's best interests. They knew she didn't want to go to Wentworth, but they also knew that she wouldn't talk to her mother about it. So they'd devised a strategy to help her get out of it. And she'd been glad to cooperate, knowing it was the easy way out. But deep down, Lisa felt horrible about putting one over on her mother. The whole thing would never have begun if she had just tried to talk to her mother. Even if her mother had insisted that Lisa look at Wentworth, Lisa should have been honest about her reaction to it.

Still, Lisa was lucky that she had the kind of friends who wouldn't rest until they had helped her. She knew she should thank them. She picked up the receiver—and put it down again. She had to talk to her mother. And that was one thing The Saddle Club couldn't help her with.

"So, YOU NEVER wanted to go to Wentworth?" Mrs. Atwood asked several hours later, her eyes searching Lisa's.

Lisa shook her head. She and her mother were sitting at the kitchen table, where they'd been for most of the evening.

"Then why didn't you say something?" Mrs. Atwood asked. "I just don't understand."

"I kept wanting to, Mom, but I knew how much you wanted me to go there and what a privilege it was supposed to be," Lisa explained, her voice threatening to crack. "It—it started with the appointment at the hair salon. I didn't want to go there, either, but I did."

Mrs. Atwood reached across the table and took Lisa's hands. "First of all, you've got to get one thing straight: I did want you to go to Wentworth, but only because I thought it would be a wonderful opportunity for you. I thought it would be something new—a challenge—and I thought it would be beneficial for you to get to know some sophisticated girls. Boarding school always sounded so glamorous to me when I was growing up." Mrs. Atwood sounded wistful. "I wanted you to have the chances I never did—meet exciting people, go to interesting places. When I heard about that scholarship, I thought it would be a dream come true. I didn't realize you didn't think it was a privilege. And I didn't realize you didn't like the girls."

"It wasn't that I didn't like them," Lisa started to protest. Then she realized she was doing it again—pretending she felt a certain way, to make her mother happy. "Okay," she admitted, "you're right. I didn't like them. In fact, I thought they were awful."

"Even that nice Sally Whitmore who showed us around?" Mrs. Atwood asked.

"*Especially* Sally Whitmore," Lisa replied.

"And she seemed so friendly and polite," Mrs. Atwood mused. "Well, all I can say is that I'm glad Barb diAngelo happened to be at Cosmo today. She sure set me straight. I hate to think that if it hadn't been for her and her daughter, you might never have told me how you felt. Promise you'll try to in the future, dear, all right?"

After Lisa promised she would, Mrs. Atwood said, "I guess we really have a lot to thank the diAngelos for, don't we?"

Lisa bit her lip. "Mom, there's something I have to say."

"Yes?" Mrs. Atwood said. "What is it?"

"I . . . I . . ." Lisa paused, thinking of the best way to explain The Saddle Club's elaborate plan. But wait—she didn't have to tell her mother *everything*, did she? "I should call Stevie and Carole soon and tell them the good news—that I'm staying put," Lisa said.

"Oh, is that all?" Mrs. Atwood said.

Lisa nodded.

"Good. Because there's something I have to say. And it concerns your future," Mrs. Atwood said gravely.

"Yes, Mom?" Lisa said.

"I insist—absolutely insist—that we keep going to the expensive hair salon," Mrs. Atwood said, starting to laugh.

"That's one privilege I'll accept!" Lisa cried.

STEVIE TOOK THE Magic Marker she was holding and contemplated throwing it at the cochair of the dance committee. Here it was, a beautiful Friday afternoon, and she was stuck staying after school to set up for the dance and finish the decorations. Those things weren't that bad. But she was stuck doing them with Veronica diAngelo! Veronica had helped save Lisa from being sent to boarding school—but did that give her the right to torture Stevie for eight days straight?

"I still think this whole fifties sock hop idea is the stupidest thing I've ever heard of," Veronica said, standing over Stevie and frowning at her work.

"Shouldn't you be setting up the food tables?" Stevie asked. She involuntarily clenched and unclenched her right hand around the marker.

"No, I'm sure the caterer will do that," Veronica replied airily.

Stevie sat back and looked up at Veronica. "The caterer?" she said.

"Well, what did you think—that I was going to make the food myself?" Veronica asked, smirking. "Very funny. I've ordered sushi . . ."

Stevie took a deep breath, said nothing, and went back to coloring in her SOCK HOP sign. *Five more hours,* she told herself. *I only have to get through five more hours with her.* It was almost three now, and the dance would start at eight.

On the brighter side, the dance committee was in pretty good shape. The gym was almost fully decorated, the stereo system was set up, kids had brought in CDs and tapes, and the parent chaperones were due to show up at seven. People at school had been talking about the dance all week, and the boys had called off their boycott.

"You know, these decorations are pretty sad," Veronica commented, looking around. "Ashley will probably think they're very public school."

Stevie rolled her eyes. That was about the millionth

122

time Veronica had mentioned her friend Ashley Briggs's visit. Stevie was beginning to feel nauseated every time she heard the name.

"I mean, couldn't you have come up with something more professional than that pretend jukebox and those silly cutouts of forty-five records?" Veronica asked.

"Sorry about that," Stevie said. "I tried to have some floats flown in from Paris, but they haven't arrived yet."

"Ha, ha," Veronica said, and sneered. Then she continued, in a sincere instead of sarcastic tone, "Oh well—even if the decorations are tacky, at least the crowd will be strictly private school."

That did it. Stevie capped her marker, stood up, and stormed out of the gym. She wasn't sure where she was going, but she knew she had to get away from Veronica. If she stayed there any longer, she'd probably do something she would later regret. Striding angrily down the hall, Stevie passed Miss Fenton's office. A few paces later, she stopped short and retraced her steps. "I've got it!" she murmured.

Ignoring the protests of Miss Fenton's secretary, Stevie rapped on the headmistress's door and marched into her office.

"Yes, Stephanie?" Miss Fenton said in a surprised voice.

"Miss Fenton, remember how you said you trusted me

to put some life into this back-to-school dance?" Stevie asked.

"Yes, I remember," Miss Fenton said, raising one eyebrow. "And?"

"Veronica is bringing her friend Ashley, and that gave me an idea. I know it's late, but if I called some people and the dance committee called some people, and *they* all called some people—"

"Yes, yes."

"—we could all invite a few friends of ours who don't go to Fenton Hall. That would really make for a great dance. Lots of new, interesting faces. And you wouldn't want Fenton Hall to be known as a snobby school, would you?"

"Certainly not. We—"

"Then say yes! Please say yes! I've got a bunch of friends who would love to come, but I couldn't ask them because the dances are always for Fenton students only."

Miss Fenton pursed her lips and looked hard at Stevie. "All right. You've got it. It's a very democratic suggestion. Now, I won't make it a precedent, but I'll say yes for this one time, and we'll see how it goes. Now make sure . . ."

Stevie didn't hear the rest. She hugged her headmistress and went skipping down the hall yelling, "Extra! Extra! Outside students invited to Fenton Hall dance!"

Miss Fenton sighed. "Make sure you get more chaperones," she called after Stevie.

STEVIE HAD NEVER seen the gym so crammed with people. She couldn't keep track of anyone—not Lisa or Carole or Phil or A.J. or Chad or Alex or her parents, who'd been pressed into chaperone service at the last minute. Everybody was wearing socks without shoes and dancing up a storm in the middle of the basketball court. On the sidelines lay hundreds of pairs of shoes.

"Stevie, you're incredible!" Lisa said, coming up with Carole to give her friend a hug. "It's packed!"

"I know. And I hope it stays that way," Stevie said. "The more people, the less chance there is of my having to see any members of my immediate family."

Carole cringed. "I know how you feel. Remember when my dad got a little overly involved at Pine Hollow?" she asked.

Stevie and Lisa nodded. Colonel Hanson had tried to help out, but he'd mostly gotten in the way. "Luckily, my parents seem to be blending into the crowd," Stevie said, craning her neck to look.

"The theme was a great idea," Lisa said. "Usually nobody dances. But they seem to like the oldies."

125

"They've got good taste," Stevie said.

The girls laughed. Stevie was known for loving all things from the fifties—records, movies, even clothes.

"What I don't get is how you talked Veronica into it," Lisa said.

"Oh, it was easy. She loved having an excuse to run out and buy a whole new fifties costume. Plus she thought it would be a big flop, and then she could tell everyone it was all my idea." Stevie grinned. "Instead it's a huge success, and it was all my idea," she said.

"Did I hear my name? Honestly, you must lead boring lives to always be talking about me," an all-too-familiar voice said.

Stevie, Lisa, and Carole spun around. Veronica was standing there with Ashley Briggs. Both of them were wearing elaborate store-bought costumes—unlike Stevie, Lisa, and Carole, who had gotten together an hour before the dance and thrown on whatever they could find in the Lakes' attic and Stevie's closet.

"Ashley, meet Stevie and Carole. I think you already know Lisa," Veronica said.

Ashley wrinkled her nose in Lisa's direction. "Do I? Oh yes. You're the girl who wanted to go to Wentworth. I'm sorry you didn't get in, but I'm sure you realize how competitive it is."

126

"Veronica," Stevie said sharply. "Is this a rumor you started?"

"Rumor?" Veronica said, playing dumb. "Yes, now that you mention it, I do recall hearing a rumor about Lisa's applying to Wentworth."

Stevie opened her mouth to protest, but Lisa stopped her. She smiled at Veronica and Ashley. "I'm sorry, too, Ashley," she said sweetly. "It would have been great to be a Wentworth girl. But, you know, I guess I just didn't have the grades."

Flustered, Veronica tried to steer Ashley away. Right then a few of the Fenton boys surrounded them. "Great dance, Stevie," one of them said.

"Yeah, especially the idea to invite outside friends," another said, with an admiring glance at Carole and Lisa.

The third one chimed in, "Everything's cool except for the food. The food is weird. No one can figure out what it is. But basically, everything's cool. And I heard you did it all by yourself."

Stevie grinned triumphantly. "That must be a rumor going around," she said.

STEVIE, LISA, AND CAROLE sat around the Atwoods'
kitchen until they were almost falling asleep at the table.
They drank tea with Mrs. Atwood; they ate cookies with
Mr. Atwood. They didn't want to go to bed. They
wanted to keep rehashing the dance. But finally they
crawled up the stairs to Lisa's bedroom.

"Lisa, I still can't believe you let Ashley Briggs think
you didn't get in to Wentworth," Carole said. She
pushed a few stuffed animals off Lisa's four-poster bed
and flopped down on it.

"It's funnier that way," Lisa said, following suit. "Besides, those girls are so stuck on themselves, they'd never believe *I* turned Wentworth down."

"*I* still can't believe Chad danced the last slow dance with Ashley Briggs," Stevie moaned, staking out space on the floor. "Of course I couldn't say anything to him. That would only make him like her more."

"It's hard when your family's involved, isn't it?" Carole said, glancing at Lisa.

"There are certain things you just can't say," Stevie agreed.

"Or at least," Lisa said, smiling, "you think you can't say them."

"So, are you glad that you spoke to your mother about Wentworth?" Carole said. Lisa had filled them in briefly on the conversation she'd had with her mother.

"I sure am," Lisa said. Then she chuckled. "I just feel bad that you had to put up with Veronica, when I should have listened to you in the first place, Stevie. I should have told my mother how I felt."

"I'll always have to put up with Veronica," Stevie responded. "The important thing is that you're staying in Willow Creek, and the dance was a success."

"I wish you two could have been at the salon when Mrs. diAngelo started in about Wentworth," Lisa said, laughing as she remembered the scene.

"So she was good, huh?" Carole asked.

"Good?" Lisa said. "She was brilliant. She gave an award-winning performance."

"Is it true that nobody is allowed to mention Wentworth in her presence?" Carole asked.

Stevie nodded. "Ashley Briggs told Chad that she can't even say the name while she's staying at Veronica's house, or Mrs. diAngelo goes crazy."

"Veronica, on the other hand, goes crazy when she hears the word *work*," Carole said.

"Now, now," Lisa said reprovingly. "As my mother said, we have a lot to thank the diAngelos for."

As Stevie and Carole went on chatting about the dance, Lisa thought back on what she'd learned in the past couple of weeks. She knew that she would never be the kind of person who told her mother everything. And she knew that it wasn't in her personality to fight with her parents. But she also knew that when it came to a subject like boarding school, she wouldn't just go along with everything, hiding her true feelings. When it came to the really important things, she would try to speak her mind.

Right now all her mind was telling her was to go to sleep. In her own bed. Where she would be sleeping for the next several years. As a day student at Willow Creek public schools. "Wild horses couldn't drag me out of bed tomorrow morning," she said, yawning loudly.

"But we've got a Horse Wise meeting," Carole pointed out. "We've got to have Starlight, Prancer, and Belle ready bright and early."

Stevie was tired. She was very tired. She was downright exhausted. But she couldn't resist a joke when she saw one. "Lisa said wild horses couldn't drag her out of bed, Carole." Stevie paused for a second before the punch line. "She didn't say anything about *tame* horses."

# ABOUT THE AUTHOR

BONNIE BRYANT is the author of many books for young readers, including novelizations of movie hits such as *Teenage Mutant Ninja Turtles* and *Honey, I Blew Up the Kid*, written under her married name, B. B. Hiller.

Ms. Bryant began writing The Saddle Club in 1986. Although she had done some riding before that, she intensified her studies then and found herself learning right along with her characters Stevie, Carole, and Lisa. She claims that they are all much better riders than she is.

Ms. Bryant was born and raised in New York City. She still lives there, in Greenwich Village, with her two sons.

Don't miss Bonnie Bryant's next exciting Saddle Club
adventure . . .

# PHANTOM HORSE
## The Saddle Club #59

Ever since strange Troy became a stable hand at Pine
Hollow, Carole's been creeped out. His scary story
about a phantom horse has made her wonder about
Starlight. Could her beloved horse really be possessed
by an evil spirit that appears once every thirteen
years? He's been acting so strange. Soon Carole's
dreams are filled with images of a red-eyed Starlight,
snorting, rearing, pawing, and ready to turn on his
owner!